Whispers in the Weave

Joceline Sparx

Whispers in the Weave © 2025 Joceline Sparx All rights reserved.

No part of this book may be copied, stored, or transmitted in any form—electronic, mechanical, photocopying, recording, or otherwise—without the express written permission of the author, except for brief quotations in reviews or articles.

This is a work of fiction. Names, characters, places, and incidents are either the product of the author's imagination or used fictitiously. Any resemblance to actual persons, living or dead, or real events is purely coincidental.

Independently Published

E-Book ISBN: 9798218611934

Print Book ISBN: 9798218625139

First Edition: March 04, 2025

For inquiries, permissions, or more information, visit: www.jocelinesparx.com

***

Step into the Weave... where love defies destiny, and even the shadows whisper of hope.

Author's Note and Content Advisories

Dedication
For the girls who feel too much, too deeply.

For the ones who have been told they are too strong, too wild, too dangerous. For those who have loved so fiercely, it left cracks in their souls. For those who have been broken, lost, or made into something they never wanted to be.

You are not beyond saving. You are not your worst mistake. You are not just the shadows that haunt you.

Even in the darkness, there is still light within you. And even the most shattered thread can be woven anew.

This story is for you.

***

"Even the brightest stars cast shadows... but even in darkness, light can still be found."

The Shadowed Enchantment Series

If you crave stories where the lines between love and darkness blur, where heroes are beautifully flawed and villains achingly human, *Shadowed Enchantments* will leave you breathless. With its perfect blend of evocative prose, smoldering romance, and thrilling adventures, this series offers an unforgettable escape into a world where magic reigns supreme and love is the most powerful enchantment of all.

Prepare to be enchanted. The shadows are waiting.

Dive into a realm where timeless fairy tales are reborn through shadows and sorcery.

Shadowed Enchantments is a captivating fourteen-book series that reimagines beloved fairy tales and iconic fantasy stories with a dark, paranormal twist. Each installment unveils a new tale of magic, mystery, and intense romance, where strong heroines navigate enchanted forests, haunted castles, and mystical realms to confront ancient curses and forbidden desires.

From the depths of the Abyssal Tides to the labyrinthine Maze of Moonlight, every story intertwines rich world-building with steamy, passionate romances that defy the boundaries of reality. Encounter fierce sorceresses, enigmatic guardians, and mythical creatures as they embark on epic quests for love, redemption, and power. Whether battling dark magic in Crimson Thorns or unraveling enchanted secrets in Unicorn's Shadow, *Shadowed Enchantments* promises an enthralling journey filled with suspense, emotion, and supernatural allure.

Perfect for fans of paranormal romance and dark fantasy, this series weaves a mesmerizing tapestry of love and magic that will keep you spellbound from the very first page to the final enchanting conclusion.

Disclaimer for *Whispers in the Weave*

This is a work of fiction. Names, characters, places, and events are either the product of the author's imagination or used fictitiously. Any resemblance to actual persons, living or dead, or real events is purely coincidental.

The magic system, mythology, and lore within *Whispers in the Weave* are unique to the world of Elysoria and are not based on any real-world beliefs, practices, or traditions.

All rights reserved. No part of this book may be copied, distributed, or reproduced in any form without the author's written permission.

Trigger Warnings

Reader discretion is advised for those sensitive to themes of fate, loss, and the blurred lines between light and darkness. This book contains themes of grief, loss, and destiny, as well as mild fantasy violence and moral dilemmas involving fate and free will. While there are romantic elements, this is a slow-burn, emotionally driven story with no explicit content.

***

Step into the Weave, where love defies destiny... and whispers of the past shape the future.

Whispers in the Weave – Official Playlist

Some love stories are written in the stars. Others unravel fate itself.

This playlist is a journey—from whispered prophecies to shattered hearts, from love that defied destiny to the darkness that took its place. These songs embody the forbidden romance, the slow fall into shadow, and the haunting echoes of what was lost.

What You'll Hear: Songs of love, longing, and impossible choices (Morganna & Aeron's bond). Dark, powerful anthems as fate tightens its grip. Villainous transformation energy as Morganna becomes Morgath. Epic cinematic tracks that capture the magic of the Weave.

Press play, step into the shadows, and let the echoes guide you...

Listen now: https://open.spotify.com/playlist/4Q6axScKtLjLJ4KFEdpzyf?si=Uc-H31f8QC-k7dJyVnA60g

***

"Some songs tell a story. Some songs whisper a fate already written. Listen closely... the Weave is never silent."

Contents

1. Prologue — 1
2. Chapter 1 — 7
3. Chapter 2 — 12
4. Chapter 3 — 31
5. Chapter 4 — 45
6. Chapter 5 — 63
7. Chapter 6 — 71
8. Chapter 7 — 81
9. Chapter 8 — 99
10. Chapter 9 — 111
11. Chapter 10 — 117
12. Chapter 11 — 125
13. Chapter 12 — 135
14. Chapter 13 — 142

15.	Chapter 14	147
16.	Chapter 15	156
17.	Chapter 16	168
18.	Chapter 17	177
19.	Chapter 18	186
20.	Epilogue	195

Prologue

"Some echoes never fade. Some shadows never rest. And some hearts refuse to be forgotten."

The fractured mirror didn't lie.

Morgath stared at the shards scattered across the stone floor, each jagged piece reflecting a different version of herself—some twisted, some beautiful, none whole. In one fragment, she was still Morganna the Luminous: golden hair cascading in molten waves, violet eyes bright with the untamed magic of the Heartstone. In another, her face was hollow and gaunt, her skin gray as ash, her pupils pinpricks swallowed by the abyss of black sclera.

But the worst reflection was the one that showed nothing at all.

She reached for it, fingers trembling as they brushed the razor edge of the glass. A sharp sting bloomed. Blood welled dark and thick from the cut, trickling down her palm like spilled ink. The shard drank it greedily, its surface rippling like disturbed water, distorting the void it held.

A voice whispered from the darkness.

Morganna.

Her breath caught, brittle as glass. No. That was impossible.

She spun around, pulse pounding in her ears, the ruined chamber suddenly too vast, too silent. Darkness pooled in the corners, not just shadows but stains—stretching, creeping, as if drawn to her warmth.

"Aeron?" The name slipped out before she could stop it.

Only silence answered.

Her fingers clenched, nails biting into the fresh wound, grounding her in the sting. It wasn't real. Just an echo—a memory stitched into the stones of this forsaken place. One of a thousand ghosts that refused to leave her.

She stepped back. Glass crunched under her boots, sharp and jarring. Her gaze drifted to the center of the chamber where the Heartstone's remains lay—jagged fragments scattered across a once-sacred altar. The stone that had pulsed with radiant light, vibrant with the essence of creation itself, now sat fractured, bled dry of all it had ever been.

Morganna had died the night it shattered. Morgath was what remained.

A slow exhale escaped her lips, thin and shaky. This chamber had once been a sanctuary—a place where the threads of fate were woven with precision, where the whispers of destiny echoed in harmony with the Heartstone's glow. Now it reeked of dust and decay, the air thick with something colder: regret, pressed into the cracked walls like frost.

She should leave. And yet, she didn't.

Her hand drifted to her wrist, to the silver-threaded bracelet still wrapped there. A braid of metal, bright and untarnished by shadow or time, unbroken. A relic from a life that no longer belonged to her. She traced it absently, remembering the warmth of his fingers fastening it there, the soft rasp of his voice: *I love you. I always have. I always will. This isn't the end for us. You'll find a way.*

His last words. His final promise.

Aeron had given his soul to the Heartstone to save her. But fate had never been kind to them. It had stolen him, ripped him away before she could whisper the truth she'd carried like a fragile ember in her chest. The truth she'd been too afraid to speak aloud.

I love you.

Now the words were ash. But ash could still burn.

She turned back to the altar, her steps slow but deliberate. Darkness gathered, not just as shadows but as folds in reality itself—thin places where the light didn't reach, where echoes of other worlds bled through. Their whispers slithered through the cold air.

Once, she would have recoiled from them. Light had been her birthright—woven into her soul, the power to shape destinies flowing through her veins like wildfire.

Now, she felt only the chill.

Morgath pressed her hand to the cold stone where the Heartstone had once blazed with life. It was silent beneath her touch, as empty as the hollow carved into her chest. Her jaw tightened. No. Not empty. Not gone.

Not forever.

She had spent years chasing whispers, hunting fragments of forgotten lore, scouring the edges of reality for anything that could undo what had been done. The Guardians had preached that fate was immutable, that the weave of time could not be unraveled once stitched.

But they were wrong.

She had seen the loose threads.

The Heartstone was not invincible. If it could be broken, it could be remade. And if it could be remade…

So could he.

A sharp wind howled through the shattered windows of the citadel, rattling the glass like brittle bones. Morgath lifted her chin, closing her eyes against the sting of cold air. In the distance, the Eclipse Bell tolled—a slow, somber chime, marking the relentless march of fate.

Once, she would have heeded its warning.

Now, she ignored it.

She turned from the altar and strode toward the open archway. Her shadow stretched behind her, long and thin, like something trying to hold on. Beyond the threshold, the Shadow Realm unfurled—an endless expanse of mist and murmurs, a place where reality's edges frayed and bled into oblivion. Once, this realm had been a prison, the boundary between light and dark, order and chaos.

Now, it was hers.

And from its depths, she would carve a new fate.

The wind shifted, carrying with it the faintest murmur—so soft she might have dismissed it as the sigh of the void itself.

Morganna.

She stilled, the sound striking like an arrow. Not an echo. Not a memory.

A whisper.

Her fingers curled into fists, her pulse quickening. If even a shred of him remained... she would find it. She would tear through the fabric of reality itself if she had to.

"When love defies where fate decrees, A golden thread shall come undone.

The Heart will break, the heavens mourn, And darkness' reign will have begun.

Born of light yet bound to Weave, A child too bright, too wild to chain.

She holds the key to all that is— Yet love will set the world aflame.

A choice will come, a cost in blood, A tether lost to time's cruel hand.

Should shadow claim a heart once pure, Then love itself will curse the land.

But echoes stir within the dark, A severed thread still sings its song.

Twelve shall rise to heal the past, And weave anew what love made wrong."

Chapter 1

"Some are born to follow the Weave. Others are born to shape it. And a rare, dangerous few—are born to break it."

The sky over Elysoria was endless.

It stretched above the Citadel in soft hues of gold and violet, the setting sun casting long shadows across the marble terraces. The spires gleamed like sharpened spears piercing the heavens, their edges etched with the runes of the Weave—ancient, eternal, and sacred.

But none of that mattered to three children racing through the narrow stone corridors, their laughter echoing off walls older than kingdoms.

Morganna was faster than both of them.

Her golden hair streamed behind her like a banner, wild and untamed, eyes gleaming with fierce determination. Aeron chased after her, his storm-gray gaze narrowing with the kind of focus that would one day make him a formidable Guardian—but today, he was just a boy trying not to lose to a girl who always seemed one step ahead.

Rhylen trailed behind, out of breath, clutching a stolen pastry he'd snagged from the Citadel kitchens. "You're cheating!" he wheezed, crumbs flying with every word.

Morganna didn't bother to look back. "I'm just better," she called over her shoulder, grinning like the troublemaker she'd always been.

They reached the training terraces at the edge of the Citadel, where the sky seemed to meet the horizon. The world beyond stretched wide—rolling hills, distant rivers, and the faint shimmer of the Weave itself, woven through the air like invisible threads waiting to be pulled.

Morganna skidded to a stop near the edge, triumphant.

Aeron arrived moments later, panting but grinning. He nudged her shoulder. "Only because you cut the corner."

"Strategy," she corrected, smug.

Rhylen collapsed onto the ground, his pastry now more crumbs than food. "I'm dying," he declared dramatically. "Tell my parents I loved them."

Morganna flopped down beside him, rolling her eyes. "You're fine." She plucked the remains of his pastry and took a bite, ignoring his outraged gasp.

Aeron sat cross-legged, looking out at the fading sun. His expression grew thoughtful, quiet in a way that always annoyed Morganna because she could never tell what he was thinking.

After a long moment, he spoke. "Do you ever wonder what it feels like to really touch the Weave?"

Morganna blinked.

"Not just through lessons or spells," Aeron added quickly, glancing at her. "But really feel it. Like... beyond what the instructors show us."

Rhylen groaned, flopping dramatically onto his back. "I barely passed my binding runes exam last week. I'm not exactly ready to have a spiritual revelation."

Morganna didn't answer.

Because she had felt it.

Not the way the instructors at the Citadel taught. Not through rituals or chants.

She had always felt it.

Like a heartbeat beneath her skin. Like invisible strings humming through the air, connecting everything—light, sound, people, fate itself.

She just... thought everyone felt it too.

Her fingers drifted to the space between her knees, hovering over the stone. She could see the faint shimmer of threads woven into the world's fabric, like golden strands hidden in plain sight.

A sudden impulse surged through her.

She reached out—

And pulled.

The world shifted.

It wasn't dramatic at first. Just a hum beneath her skin, a resonance like striking the right note on a stringed instrument. The air grew heavier, charged with something unseen, as if the sky itself had paused to watch. Then—

A breeze shot across the terrace, sharp and sudden, scattering Rhylen's crumbs and whipping Aeron's hair into his face. The ground beneath them thrummed, a pulse of energy rippling outward like a stone dropped in water.

She felt a whisper at the edge of her mind, slight but there. Morganna froze. So did the boys.

Rhylen scrambled upright, eyes wide. "What the hell was that?!"

Morganna stared at her hands. They weren't glowing—not exactly. But the air around them shimmered faintly, like heat waves rising from stone. Her heart raced, not with fear, but something sharper. Like standing on the edge of a cliff and realizing she wanted to jump just to see if she could fly.

Aeron didn't speak right away. His storm-gray eyes met hers, and for the first time, there was something new in them. Not fear. Not confusion.

Recognition.

"Morganna, I think, I think you pulled the Weave," he whispered.

Morganna swallowed hard. "I didn't mean to."

But that was a lie. She had meant to. She'd just never thought it would actually work.

Rhylen waved his hands dramatically. "Wait, wait, wait. She did what? You can't just say 'pulled the Weave' like that's normal!"

But Aeron wasn't listening. He was still staring at Morganna, his brow furrowed like he was trying to solve a puzzle no one had given him the pieces for.

"It responded to you," he murmured. "Like... like it knew you."

Morganna didn't know what to say.

Because deep down, she'd always known she was different. The way magic felt too easy sometimes, the way she could finish spells before the instructors had even finished explaining them. The way the Weave wasn't something she learned to touch—

It was something that had always been waiting for her.

Rhylen crossed his arms, clearly unimpressed with this revelation. "So, what? Is she magic or something? We're all magic. That's the point of being a Guardian."

Aeron shook his head slowly, his voice softer now, like he was speaking a truth he'd only just realized.

"No," he said. "She's not just magic."

He hesitated, amazed and yet confused. How was it possible? He struggled to find the words, how to explain what he thought. Then, with a certainty that sent a chill down Morganna's spine, he added:

"She is the Weave."

The words settled over them like dust—light and heavy all at once.

Morganna's chest tightened. She didn't know what that meant. She didn't want to know.

So she did what she always did when things got too big, too heavy.

She laughed, but she gave away her stress with the clenching of her fists.

"Great," she said, standing up and dusting off her hands. "Guess that means I'm destined for something dramatic and tragic."

Rhylen snorted. "Probably involving a prophecy."

But Aeron didn't laugh. He just smiled faintly, shaking his head.

"Or maybe," he said quietly, "you're meant to change the world."

Morganna rolled her eyes. "Yeah, well—let's start with changing the fact that Rhylen owes me another pastry."

She took off running again, her laughter echoing across the terraces.

Rhylen cursed and sprinted after her, shouting something about unfair advantages.

Aeron lingered a moment longer, staring at the spot where she'd pulled the Weave. The faint shimmer still lingered there, like the world itself had been marked by her touch.

Eventually, he smiled to himself and ran after them.

But the words he'd spoken stayed behind.

A simple truth woven into the threads of fate.

She's meant to change the world.

And someday— She would.

Chapter 2

"Fate binds us all—but some threads are woven tighter than others."

The sky above Starfall Citadel burned with the soft glow of dusk, streaked with hues of violet and gold, as if the Weave itself had stitched the colors into place. Wisps of amber clouds drifted lazily across the horizon, bleeding into the deepening indigo of approaching night. From the high cliffs, the sprawling world of Elysoria stretched endlessly—forests dark and ancient like tangled knots of emerald thread, rivers flashing silver in the dying light, winding through the land like veins beneath the skin of the world.

But none of that mattered. Not today.

Not when Rhylen and Aeron were trying to kill each other.

Well—not literally. Probably.

Morganna sat cross-legged on the crumbling stone wall overlooking the Guardian training grounds, her chin resting lazily on her palm. The evening breeze carried the crisp bite of autumn, tugging at strands of her golden hair and whispering through the ancient banners that hung limp against the citadel's worn stone towers. She barely noticed.

Her eyes were fixed on the familiar scene below—the clash of steel against steel, the gleam of sweat on determined faces, the echo of footsteps pounding against hard-packed earth.

She'd lost count of how many times she'd witnessed this exact moment: Aeron's sharp grin flashing like a blade, Rhylen's silent intensity etched into the tight line of his jaw. They moved like echoes of themselves, locked in a dance that was equal parts battle and ballet.

They'd been friends for as long as she could remember, though *friends* felt too small a word to contain what the three of them were. Tangled threads, maybe—knotted together by fate, by duty, by something deeper and infinitely more complicated.

Aeron moved like the wind—quick, unpredictable, impossible to catch. His gray eyes sparkled with mischief, even in the midst of combat, as if the whole thing were a game only he understood. He dodged one of Rhylen's strikes with infuriating ease, twisting his dagger just out of reach, his laughter carried on the breeze.

Rhylen was the opposite—solid as stone, grounded in precision and discipline. His movements were measured, every strike deliberate, his strength not in speed but in stubborn, relentless control. He fought like he did everything else: with his whole heart, even if he'd never admit it.

And Aeron? Aeron fought like he had nothing to lose. Which was ridiculous. He had everything to lose.

"You're slowing down, Rhy!" Aeron's voice rang out, smug and breathless, a grin tugging at the corner of his mouth.

Rhylen's only reply was a grunt and a low sweep of his leg, aiming to knock Aeron off balance.

Aeron leapt over it with maddening ease, flipping backward to land light as air, his boots barely stirring dust. *Show-off.*

Morganna rolled her eyes, unable to hide her smirk. "If either of you spent half as much time studying as you do trying to bruise each other, you'd both be Grandmasters by now."

Aeron flashed her a grin, sweat gleaming at his temples. "And miss this? Absolutely not."

Rhylen barked a short laugh, pausing to wipe his forearm across his face. "She's just mad we're better with blades than she is."

"Oh, please." Morganna slid off the wall in one smooth motion, landing with the grace of someone born to defy gravity. She strolled toward them, her eyes alight with challenge. "I could flatten both of you without breaking a sweat."

Aeron arched a brow, spinning his dagger lazily between his fingers. "Is that a challenge?"

She tilted her head, a sly smile curving her lips. "It's a promise."

The tension between them was like a thread pulled taut—always there, humming with something unsaid, vibrating beneath every glance, every word.

Rhylen glanced between them, his sharp gaze catching the flicker of something more in Aeron's grin, in Morganna's half-lidded eyes. A knowing smirk tugged at his mouth, but there was something else behind it this time—something quieter. Not jealousy, exactly, but… distance.

He masked it quickly. He always did. But Morganna saw it.

He knows. Everyone knew.

But Guardians weren't supposed to love. Not like that. Not when fate was fragile enough without tangled hearts getting in the way.

***

Later, after the sun dipped below the horizon and the sky was stitched with stars, Aeron found her alone.

Morganna sat at the cliff's edge, her knees pulled to her chest, staring out over the endless expanse below. The distant lights of scattered villages flickered like fragile embers, tiny sparks defying the vast darkness. The wind carried the faint scent of ash and wildflowers—bittersweet and fleeting, like everything she tried to hold onto these days.

The Weave felt quieter at night—or maybe it was just easier to pretend she couldn't hear it humming beneath her skin, pulling her toward destinies she wasn't ready to face.

Without a word, Aeron dropped down beside her, close enough that their shoulders brushed. He smelled of steel and sweat, layered with something faintly like cedar smoke and worn leather—familiar, grounding, like the echo of a memory she never wanted to forget.

They didn't speak at first. They never needed to. The silence between them was never empty; it was filled with all the things they couldn't say.

Eventually, Aeron reached into his pocket, his fingers hesitating for the briefest moment before he pulled out something small—delicate. A thin bracelet woven from silver thread, its intricate strands catching the faint light of the crescent moon. A small, star-shaped charm dangled from it, crafted from the same enchanted silver. But the star wasn't solid—it was hollow at the center, as if Aeron had carved out the heart of it, leaving a space that felt both empty and full at the same time.

Inside the hollow space was a tiny crystal shard. It gleamed softly, fragile yet strong, as if it had been stitched from starlight itself.

Morganna tilted her head, curiosity flickering behind her violet eyes. "What's that?"

He didn't meet her gaze at first. His thumb brushed over the threads, his expression unusually serious. "Something I made for you."

Her heart stumbled, a small, traitorous skip. She reached out slowly, her fingers grazing his as she took it. The bracelet was warm—not from the lingering heat of his skin, but from something deeper. It pulsed softly with magic. His magic.

She swallowed, her throat tightening against words she didn't know how to shape. "Aeron..."

"I infused it," he murmured, his voice quieter than she'd ever heard it, like he was afraid the night might steal the words away. "Just a sliver of my magic. It'll protect you... if I'm not there."

The words hit harder than any blade could.

She wanted to laugh, to tease him, to break the fragile tension with some careless quip—the way they always did. But the words wouldn't come.

Because she knew why he'd made it. Because he loved her. And because he couldn't say it.

Not when the rules carved it into stone: Guardians do not have relationships. They do not fall in love.

But fate didn't get to carve everything.

Her fingers trembled slightly as she held the bracelet, feeling the warmth seep into her skin like sunlight trying to reach her through clouds. She turned to him, her voice softer now, stripped of its usual armor. "Thank you," she whispered, the simplicity of the words carrying more weight than either of them expected.

Aeron's breath hitched, the barest flicker of surprise flashing across his face, quickly masked by a crooked smile. "Here, let me."

He took the bracelet gently from her hands, his fingers brushing against her wrist as he fastened it. His touch was light, careful, as if she were made of something fragile, something precious. But it wasn't just his magic woven into the threads—it was him, stitched between every fiber, every knot.

As his fingers lingered against her skin, Morganna closed her eyes, letting the connection hum between them like a taut thread pulled between two distant stars. Then, without hesitation, she reached inward—past the walls she'd built, past the fear—and poured the smallest sliver of herself into the bracelet.

A piece of her soul.

A spark of violet light flickered beneath his fingertips, fading as quickly as it had come, sinking into the threads like a heartbeat finding its rhythm.

Aeron's eyes shot to hers, wide with surprise, a question unspoken on his lips.

But she answered before he could ask.

"Guardians aren't allowed to be together," she said softly, her voice steady despite the storm in her chest. She lifted her wrist, the bracelet glinting faintly between them, more than silver now—more than magic. A promise. "But in this, we will be together. Always."

Aeron didn't speak. He couldn't. The words were too big to fit between breaths.

But the look in his eyes—the way his fingers tightened around hers, as if he could anchor her to this moment, to him—said everything.

His smile was softer this time, but it reached his eyes, burning brighter than any star above them.

"Always," he whispered.

And somewhere in the distance, fate listened.

***

The next morning, Morganna woke with a start.

Something was wrong.

She felt it in her bones, like a splinter embedded too deep to see. The Weave thrummed with an unfamiliar tension—a thread pulled too tight, fraying at the edges, ready to snap.

The sky was too bright, the colors too sharp, as if the world itself was holding its breath.

She found Aeron and Rhylen back in the training grounds, blades flashing under the pale morning sun. But the air felt... different.

The way Aeron's grin didn't linger. The way Rhylen's eyes flicked toward the horizon, sharp and distant. The way her heart beat too fast, for no reason she could name.

Because this wasn't just a ripple in the Weave. It was the start of something unraveling. And none of them were ready for what was coming.

***

The Weave hummed beneath Morganna's fingertips, pulsing with life.

It was like touching the heartbeat of the universe—delicate yet vast, an endless tapestry of threads spun from light, shadow, and something older than either. Each strand glowed with its own hue: gold for strength, silver for wisdom, blue for the immutable flow of fate, red for passion, and threads so dark they seemed to swallow light, representing choices best left untouched.

With a thought, Morganna wove them into harmony, her magic flowing like a song only she could hear—a melody threaded through the very fabric of existence. The strands responded to her effortlessly, bending and twisting with the grace of a river guided by its banks.

She breathed it in. This was her power. This was her gift. And today, it was hers alone to wield.

The chamber of the Heartstone stretched around her, vast and echoing, carved from crystalline walls that refracted the threads of magic into shifting prisms of color. The light danced like ghosts across the polished floor, a mosaic of ever-changing hues.

At the center stood the Heartstone itself—an enormous gem pulsing with faint, rhythmic light, as though it too had a heartbeat that answered her own.

Morganna exhaled slowly, her breath visible in the cool air, and extended her hand. The threads of fate quivered, trembling beneath her will. She guided them with precision, fingers flicking in small, deliberate gestures, weaving a pattern intricate enough to challenge even the most skilled of Guardians.

Just one more piece...

She reached deeper, beyond the shallow threads of simple magic, diving into the hidden layers where reality itself was stitched together. She sought the pulse beneath the pulse, the thread that didn't belong—the one that would complete her pattern.

Her fingers brushed it.

And the Weave stuttered.

Morganna stiffened, her breath catching in her throat. A cold shiver traced her spine, sharp and sudden. That had never happened before. The Weave was supposed to be seamless—fluid, perfect. Fate didn't hesitate. Its patterns were immutable, its course set long before mortals ever dared to glimpse it.

She tried again, this time with more focus, her brow furrowing in concentration. But the thread unraveled in her grip, slipping through her fingers like smoke. No—like sand, slipping faster the tighter she tried to hold it.

What the—

Morganna!

The voice hit her like a shockwave—sharp, familiar, laced with both frustration and concern.

Before she could react, a strong, calloused hand gripped her wrist, yanking her back with surprising force. The threads snapped away from her touch like a recoiling serpent, vanishing into the ether.

She whirled around, golden hair flaring like a banner, ready to unleash a scathing retort—only to find herself face-to-face with piercing storm-gray eyes.

Aeron.

Aether Weaver. Guardian. Her partner. Her opposite. The only person who had ever been able to keep up with her.

He stood close, his dark brow arched in silent judgment, a faint crease between his eyes betraying his worry. The faint glow of residual magic crackled at his fingertips before fading, his grip on her wrist loosening but not falling away entirely.

"What exactly do you think you're doing?" he asked, his voice low but firm, threaded with exasperation.

Morganna huffed, yanking her arm free, ignoring the faint warmth his touch had left behind. "Working, obviously."

"Looked more like you were tempting fate."

She shot him a glare. "*I am* fate." She gestured toward the lingering threads still flickering faintly in the air around them, remnants of the pattern she'd been weaving. "That's literally my job."

Aeron crossed his arms, his broad frame casting a shadow that seemed to swallow the fractured light. His magic—cool, steady, and utterly different from her own—rippled beneath the surface of his composed exterior. Where Morganna was wildfire, untamed and brilliant, Aeron was stone—unmoving, unyielding, carved by duty and sharpened by discipline.

"And mine," he replied evenly, "is keeping you from tearing a hole in reality."

Morganna rolled her eyes, though her heart was still racing. "You're being dramatic."

He wasn't. And they both knew it.

Aeron stepped closer, the charged space between them narrowing until she could feel the faint thrum of his magic brushing against hers—like opposite currents colliding, never fully merging. His gaze softened slightly, the sharp edges dulled by something more vulnerable.

"What did you see?"

She hesitated. The words stuck in her throat, reluctant to be spoken aloud, as if naming the wrongness would give it power. Morganna had spent years unraveling the Weave, mastering its complexity, perfecting her craft with a confidence that bordered on arrogance.

But today—just for a moment—it had slipped beyond her control. She didn't like that.

Her gaze drifted to the Heartstone. Its glow seemed dimmer now, the rhythm of its pulse slightly off, like a heartbeat with an uneven skip.

"I don't know," she admitted quietly, the confession tasting bitter. "Something was... wrong."

Aeron didn't scoff. He didn't dismiss her like the other Guardians might have, with their rigid doctrines and blind faith in the stability of fate. He just waited, patient as always, steady as the anchor he'd been since the first day they met.

That was the thing about Aeron. He never told her she was imagining things.

She swallowed the lump forming in her throat. "The Weave... hesitated."

His expression darkened, the faint crease between his brows deepening. "That's never happened before."

"No."

They stood in silence, the weight of her words settling between them like a fragile glass thread, one breath away from shattering.

Morganna forced a smile, brittle at the edges, trying to shake the unease curling in her gut. "It's probably nothing. Just a fluke."

Aeron didn't look convinced. His gaze drifted back to the Heartstone, then to the faint, fading echoes of the threads she'd been weaving.

"Or it's the start of something worse."

The way he said it—quiet, certain, like a blade sliding between armor—sent another shiver through her.

She wanted to dismiss it. She wanted to roll her eyes, to call him paranoid. The Weave didn't just break. It wasn't supposed to.

But she had felt it. And so had he.

***

Morganna exhaled sharply, raking a hand through her hair. "Fine. I'll check the Weave again later. But if it was a fluke..."—she forced a teasing edge into her voice, trying to lighten the air—"you owe me dinner."

Aeron's lips quirked into a smirk, though it didn't fully reach his eyes. "You wish."

For a heartbeat, the tension cracked, a spark of warmth flickering between them—the same unspoken challenge they'd danced around for years.

Duty first. Always.

But beneath the banter, the unease remained, coiled like a sleeping serpent.

Morganna turned back to the Heartstone, the dim pulse of its light reflecting in her violet eyes. She reached for the threads again, but the certainty she'd always carried felt just a little farther out of reach.

If fate had truly hesitated... What did that mean for the future?

***

Aeron followed her out of the chamber, his footsteps echoing softly against the smooth crystal floor. The faint, rhythmic sound blended with the ambient hum of the Citadel's magic, like a heartbeat woven into the walls themselves.

He moved with the same effortless grace he always did—silent, deliberate, like a shadow that had learned how to walk among the light. Morganna hated how comforting his presence could be, even when he was insufferably annoying. There was something steady about him, like the constant pull of gravity—unchanging, unavoidable.

The corridor opened into the heart of the Citadel of Balance, a breathtaking expanse of towering arches and skybridges suspended in impossible elegance above an endless sea of stars. The Citadel had been built at the very edge of reality itself, where the Weave was at its most stable—or at least, it had been.

Today, the stars seemed restless.

Their light flickered with an uneasy rhythm, like candles trembling in a wind only they could feel. Constellations she'd traced since childhood felt unfamiliar, their patterns subtly wrong, as if the sky itself had shifted when she wasn't looking.

Morganna forced herself to ignore it.

"You're quiet," Aeron said, falling into step beside her, his voice breaking the fragile silence.

She shrugged, eyes fixed ahead. "Just thinking."

"Dangerous," he replied with a crooked grin.

"Shut up."

His chuckle was low, warm, and entirely unfair. It curled around her like a blanket she hadn't asked for but couldn't bring herself to throw off. She shot him a sideways glance, trying—and failing—not to smile.

Aeron had that effect on her.

She risked another glance, taking in the way his dark hair fell messily across his forehead, slightly damp from the humidity lingering in the air. His sharp jaw was dusted with the faintest shadow of stubble, a detail she tried not to notice but always did. His storm-gray eyes, flecked with hints of silver, seemed to catch everything—like they could peel back layers of her thoughts she'd rather keep hidden.

Too much.

He caught her looking and raised an eyebrow, one corner of his mouth tilting upward.

"What?"

"Nothing," she muttered, quickening her pace to hide the faint flush creeping up her neck. She hoped he wouldn't press.

He didn't.

Instead, he let the silence stretch between them, comfortable in a way only years of partnership could create. The kind of silence that wasn't empty but filled with all the things that didn't need to be said.

They'd been paired together since she was fourteen—barely more than a child by Guardian standards, though she'd never felt like one. Not with the weight of destiny stitched into the very fabric of her being.

Aeron at sixteen, an Aether Weaver, assigned to be her partner, her anchor. It made him more serious, following the rules and making sure she was always behaving. She'd hated him for it at first. He was too serious, too stubborn, too... everything. Too good at standing in her way.

And now? Now, he was the only person who understood what it meant to carry that weight.

The corridor ended at the edge of the Citadel, where a wide balcony jutted out into open nothingness. The railings were carved from luminous stone, etched with ancient runes that pulsed faintly in the moonlight. Morganna leaned against the cool metal, letting the night air brush against her skin.

Below, the stars stretched endlessly—an ocean of fractured glass scattered across the void. The edge of reality blurred where the darkness met the light, and for a moment, she wondered if the stars had always felt so... fragile.

"Do you ever wonder what's out there?" she asked quietly, her voice barely more than a whisper.

Aeron joined her, resting his arms on the railing, his shoulder brushing against hers. The contact was subtle, casual, but it sent an inexplicable warmth spiraling through her chest.

"Beyond the Weave?" he asked.

"Yeah."

He was quiet for a beat, his gaze distant. "Nothing good, probably."

She huffed a soft laugh. "Helpful."

"Hey, you asked."

She smiled despite herself, but it didn't last. The laughter faded, replaced by the lingering shadow of unease. Her thoughts drifted back to the chamber—to the threads slipping through her fingers, to the way the Weave had hesitated.

It wasn't supposed to do that.

Aeron's voice was softer when he spoke again. "You're still thinking about it."

She nodded, her fingers tightening slightly around the railing. "Something's wrong, Aeron. I can feel it."

"I know."

That was the thing about him. He never told her she was overreacting. Never dismissed her fears the way the other Guardians did with polite indifference and empty reassurances. Aeron listened. He believed her, even when she didn't believe herself.

Her chest tightened. "What if..." She hesitated, the words catching like thorns in her throat. "What if it's more than just a fluke?"

"Then we'll figure it out."

It was such a simple answer. So Aeron. He made everything sound easy, as if fate itself could be bent with sheer stubbornness and the strength of his belief.

But fate didn't work that way.

She sighed, brushing a loose strand of hair behind her ear, her fingers lingering near the silver-threaded bracelet on her wrist. She could still feel the faint pulse of magic woven into it—his magic, and a sliver of her own. A promise etched into something small enough to be forgotten, but impossible to ignore.

"You make it sound like that's something we can control," she said quietly.

"Maybe we can't," he admitted. "But you're not facing it alone."

His words were simple, but they landed like a weight in her chest—warm, heavy, grounding. She wanted to believe him. She wanted to believe that whatever was coming, they could handle it the way they always had—together.

But deep down, she knew better.

***

The wind shifted, carrying with it the faintest murmur—so soft she thought she imagined it.

Morganna stiffened, her hand instinctively going to the bracelet on her wrist. The warmth of it pulsed faintly against her skin, steady but fragile, like a heartbeat too far away to reach.

The breeze died as quickly as it had come, leaving only silence in its wake.

"Did you hear that?" she asked, her voice low, sharp around the edges.

Aeron frowned, his gaze sweeping the balcony, his posture subtly shifting—alert, ready. "Hear what?"

She shook her head, trying to chase the chill from her spine. "Nothing."

But it wasn't nothing. It had been a voice. Soft. Faint. A whisper carried on the wind.

Her name.

Morganna stood motionless, her heart pounding like a drum against the cage of her ribs.

The whisper had been faint, almost lost in the wind—soft as breath, fragile as ash. But she knew what she'd heard.

Her name. Not spoken. Not shouted. Just... breathed into existence, as if the universe itself had exhaled her essence into the air.

She swallowed hard, casting a quick glance at Aeron. His face was carved with concern, his storm-gray eyes narrowed, searching her expression for clues she couldn't give. But there was no recognition in his gaze.

He hadn't heard it.

Which meant either she was imagining things, or— No. She wasn't imagining it.

Morganna closed her eyes, steadying her breath. She reached out—not with her hands, but with something deeper, something older than language. Magic pulsed outward from the center of her chest, like a ripple across still water, seeking the invisible threads that wove the world together.

The Weave.

She expected it to feel smooth and fluid, its patterns seamless, flowing with the effortless grace of fate's design. That was how it had always felt—constant, unbreakable.

But today...

Today, she felt the jagged edges of something torn.

It was like brushing her fingers over shattered glass, the threads frayed and brittle, as if reality itself had been stretched too thin and was beginning to tear.

Her breath caught in her throat.

"Aeron," she whispered, her voice barely more than a thread itself.

The moment his name left her lips, the Weave shuddered.

It was subtle—like the world inhaling sharply, the stars above flickering erratically as if the sky itself had been startled awake. The ground beneath her feet felt suddenly distant, as though gravity had loosened its grip, just for a heartbeat.

Then, as quickly as it had come, it was gone.

The sensation, the unraveling—vanished, like it had never been there at all.

But it had been.

She opened her eyes to find Aeron watching her, his expression sharpened by something colder than concern.

He didn't ask what had happened. He didn't need to.

"You felt something," he said quietly, his voice a steady anchor against the storm building inside her.

Morganna nodded, her chest tight. "Something's broken."

The words felt heavier once spoken, like admitting them had given them weight, given them power.

The wind picked up again, colder this time, howling through the open-air balcony with a sharp, biting edge. But it wasn't just the wind. There was something in it—an undercurrent, dark and unnatural, like a whisper woven into the breeze.

Aeron felt it too. He had grown attuned to Morganna and the weave, he felt it in his soul that something was wrong.

She noticed his reaction in the way his shoulders tensed, the subtle shift in his stance as instinct kicked in. His magic responded without him having to call it, crackling faintly in the air around him. Unlike Morganna's connection to fate's threads, Aeron's gift was raw—a force drawn from the Aether itself, bending the unseen currents of existence to his will.

If even his magic reacted... That meant whatever was wrong wasn't just in her head.

"Come on," Aeron said, his voice low but urgent. He was already moving, his stride quick and sure, the kind of pace that didn't allow for argument. "We're telling the High Council."

For once, Morganna didn't argue.

She could pretend this was nothing. She could dismiss it like the other Guardians always did when the world felt strange around the edges. She could tell herself fate was as unshakable as it had always been.

But that would be a lie.

And fate had already hesitated once today.

Chapter 3

"The greatest secrets are not hidden in shadow, but in plain sight—guarded by those who fear what would happen if the truth were known."

The Chamber of the High Council was impossibly vast, carved from black stone veined with threads of pure starlight. The ceiling stretched so high it disappeared into shadow, punctuated only by faint, floating orbs of light that pulsed in slow rhythm—like the chamber itself was breathing.

Twelve thrones formed a perfect circle at the room's center, crafted from crystal and etched with runes older than any living Guardian. In the middle, suspended above a shallow well of reflective obsidian, floated the Heartstone. It pulsed faintly, its light once radiant but now dim, flickering like a dying star.

Morganna felt it before she crossed the threshold—a heaviness pressing against her chest, as if the very air resisted her presence.

She and Aeron entered without ceremony. They were late, but that hardly mattered now.

The Guardians of Balance were already gathered, their robes cascading like waterfalls of dark silk, embroidered with symbols of their rank and power. Their faces were masks—carefully composed, expressions carved from stone. Some looked up with mild curiosity. Others with thinly veiled irritation at the interruption.

But it was the figure seated at the head of the circle that made Morganna's pulse quicken.

Grandmaster Eryndor.

His presence was as immovable as a mountain, his silvered beard and weathered face etched with the wisdom—and scars—of centuries. His eyes, sharp and unyielding, pinned them both with the weight of expectation. Morganna had spent her entire life trying to earn his approval.

Right now, she didn't care if she had it or not.

Aeron didn't wait for permission to speak. His voice cut through the chamber like a blade.

"Something is wrong with the Weave."

The effect was immediate.

Murmurs rippled through the Council like a wave, soft but sharp-edged—skepticism, curiosity, fear, all woven together beneath the surface.

Eryndor raised a single hand, and the room fell into silence. His gaze shifted to Morganna, piercing and cold. "Explain."

She stepped forward, squaring her shoulders, refusing to let her voice waver. "I felt it shift today. The threads of fate—they hesitated. Like something was pulling at them from the other side."

The words hung in the air, fragile as glass.

Silence.

Eryndor's expression didn't change. He turned to the Oracle, the youngest member of the Council. His pale green eyes were clouded with the faint, iridescent sheen of Sight, his thin frame almost lost within the folds of his ceremonial robes.

"Do you confirm this?" Eryndor asked.

The Oracle hesitated—just for a fraction of a second. But Morganna saw it.

A faint twitch of his fingers, like he was suppressing a tremor. A flicker of magic behind his iridescent eyes, gone before it fully formed. Fear.

It was gone as quickly as it appeared, replaced by the calm mask all Oracles were trained to wear.

"I have seen no disruptions in the Weave," he said carefully as he looked in Morganna's directions and then away quickly, each word weighed and measured. Morganna stiffened.

Liar.

She'd trained under the Oracle. She knew the subtle shifts in his voice, the way his gaze darted almost imperceptibly to the floor when he wasn't telling the whole truth.

He had seen something. He was choosing not to speak it aloud.

Her hands clenched at her sides, nails digging into her palms.

Eryndor's gaze lingered on the Oracle for a heartbeat longer, then turned back to Morganna and Aeron. "Then we will not act on shadows. The Weave is intact. That is the end of this discussion."

Morganna's jaw tightened. She opened her mouth to argue, but Aeron's hand was suddenly at her wrist—a silent warning.

Not now.

She gritted her teeth but obeyed, even as the words she wanted to scream burned in her throat.

The Weave is intact.

Then why did it feel like it was already unraveling beneath her feet?

***

Morganna stormed down the narrow stone corridor, her boots striking the floor with sharp, angry echoes. Sparks of uncontrolled magic crackled at her fingertips, leaving faint trails of light in the dark.

"They know something is wrong," she snapped, her voice a sharp edge against the silence. "They're just too afraid to say it."

Aeron followed, his expression unreadable—the same frustrating calm he always wore when she wanted to scream. "Maybe."

She whirled on him, her magic flaring brighter for just a heartbeat. "*Maybe?* You heard the Oracle. He lied."

Aeron exhaled slowly, running a hand through his hair. "I know."

The simple acknowledgment stopped her in her tracks. She blinked. "Then why didn't you say anything?"

His jaw tightened. "Because if they aren't admitting it, there's a reason."

She hated that he was right.

The Guardians never ignored signs of fate shifting. If they were pretending nothing was wrong, that meant whatever they had seen was something they didn't want to face.

Something worse than a simple unraveling.

Morganna let out a shaky breath, the fury slowly cooling into something colder—fear. "So what do we do?"

Aeron didn't answer right away. His eyes darkened, the storm clouds gathering behind them. Then, in a voice far too calm for what he was suggesting, he said:

"We find the truth ourselves."

Her heart skipped a beat. "You mean break the rules."

A faint, familiar smirk tugged at the corner of his mouth. "You love breaking the rules."

And maybe she did. But this felt different.

Because if the Council was wrong—if they were hiding something—then the unraveling had already begun. And this time, fate wasn't going to fix itself.

***

They didn't speak as they left the Council chambers, but the silence between them wasn't empty. It was charged.

The polished stone corridors of the Citadel echoed with the faint, rhythmic sound of their footsteps, each one falling in perfect step with the other—a habit born of years spent side by side. But tonight, the familiar cadence felt heavier, like the echoes themselves were pressing in on them, amplifying the words they didn't say.

Morganna could still feel the ghost of Aeron's fingers around her wrist, the way his grip had tightened—not enough to hurt, just enough to hold her back. The way he always held her back when she burned too hot, when she was ready to throw herself into the fire just to prove she couldn't be consumed by it.

But the truth was, it made her reckless. *He* made her reckless. It made her want things she couldn't have.

They turned a corner, the high-vaulted corridors of the Citadel stretching out before them, empty at this late hour. Starlight spilled through tall, crystalline windows, casting fractured beams across the marble floors. The soft glow painted Aeron's face in sharp contrasts—light and shadow dancing across the hard angles of his jaw, the faint crease between his brows etched deeper than usual.

She hated when he did that—locked himself behind that unreadable mask, shutting her out with nothing more than silence and the stubborn set of his jaw. She wanted to crack him open, to see what was buried beneath the surface, beneath all the rules and carefully constructed walls.

So, she broke the silence the only way she knew how.

"You were going to say something in there," she said, her voice cutting through the stillness like a blade. "To the Oracle."

Aeron sighed, scrubbing a hand over the back of his neck, his fingers raking through his dark hair. "Yeah. And it wouldn't have helped."

Morganna stopped walking, planting herself in the middle of the corridor. "You don't know that."

He turned to face her fully, the starlight catching in his storm-gray eyes, turning them to molten silver. "Yes, I do. They've already made up their minds. No matter what we say, they won't listen."

She hated that he was right.

Her arms crossed instinctively, fingers tapping a restless rhythm against the fabric of her sleeves. "Then we should—"

"—figure it out on our own," he finished for her, his lips twitching into a faint smirk. "I know."

Morganna arched a brow. "You sound awfully eager to break Guardian law."

Aeron stepped closer, slow and deliberate, like gravity itself had decided to pull him toward her. The space between them shrank until there was nothing but the faintest breath of air. His presence was overwhelming—warm, despite the cool corridor, his magic humming just beneath his skin like a storm waiting to break.

"You bring out the worst in me," he murmured, voice low, rough around the edges.

It wasn't the first time he'd said something like that. But it was the way he said it now—like a confession wrapped in a challenge.

Her pulse quickened, heat coiling low in her chest.

She should step back. Create space. But she didn't.

Instead, she held his gaze, searching for something—anything—that would give him away. A crack in the armor, a flicker of vulnerability, a sign that she wasn't the only one standing too close to the edge of something dangerous.

Give me a reason to cross the line, she wanted to say. But she didn't.

Because there was always a line. And crossing it meant losing everything.

They were Guardians of Balance. Bound by fate, by duty, by oaths carved into the foundation of the very world they protected. Love—*this*—was a fracture in the perfect symmetry they were sworn to uphold.

And yet...

His breath was uneven, just the slightest hitch in the space between heartbeats. She could see the flecks of silver in his irises, could feel the faint hum of his magic, not chaotic like hers but steady, grounding.

Like maybe—just maybe—he was thinking the same thing she was.

Morganna swallowed hard. Her voice, when it came, was softer than she meant it to be. "You should go."

Aeron didn't move. Instead, he reached out—slowly, like he was afraid of breaking something fragile—and his fingers brushed against the silver-threaded bracelet wrapped around her wrist.

The one he'd given her years ago.

His touch was feather-light, barely there, but it sent a shiver racing up her arm, a cascade of warmth she couldn't blame on magic.

"You still wear it," he murmured, his thumb tracing the silver threads with an absent, familiar motion.

Morganna closed her eyes for half a second, steadying herself. When she opened them, her smile was forced into place like armor. "Of course I do."

His thumb paused over the silver charm, his gaze darkening just a shade. "Why?"

The question wasn't casual. It wasn't rhetorical. It mattered.

Her throat tightened.

Because it's yours. Because it's the only piece of you I'm allowed to keep. Because it reminds me that someone once promised I'd never be alone.

But she didn't say any of that.

Instead, she lifted her chin, forcing a smirk. "It looks good on me."

Aeron huffed a quiet laugh, shaking his head. "Of course that's your answer."

And just like that, the moment passed. She hated how easily he could pull away, how effortlessly he tucked all those unspoken things back into the neat little box where they kept everything forbidden.

He stepped back, the warmth of him vanishing with the space between them. The chill that filled its place felt like a hollow echo.

"We should get some sleep," he said, his voice carefully neutral. "Tomorrow, we start digging."

Morganna let out a slow breath, nodding even though her chest felt too tight. "Yeah. Tomorrow."

They parted ways without another word.

But that night, as she lay awake in her chambers, staring at the ceiling painted with constellations older than memory, she replayed every second of that moment—his voice, his touch, the weight of his gaze.

She'd spent years pretending none of it meant anything. That *they* didn't mean anything.

But for the first time in years, she wasn't sure she wanted to keep pretending at all. And maybe... Maybe he didn't want to pretend either.

***

Morganna didn't go to her chambers. She should have. She should've done a thousand things—meditated, rested, prepared for whatever was unraveling beneath the fragile threads of the Weave.

But instead, her feet carried her somewhere else. Somewhere familiar.

The training terraces.

The sky stretched wide and open above them, an ocean of darkness scattered with stars—cold, distant, indifferent. The terraces were carved from pale stone, smooth from centuries of footfalls, bordered by edges that overlooked the abyss beyond the Citadel's floating spires. The faint hum of the Weave was quieter here, almost as if the threads themselves were holding their breath.

She wasn't surprised when she heard footsteps behind her.

Aeron.

"You couldn't sleep either," he said, falling into step beside her, his voice low and steady, carrying just enough warmth to crack the silence.

Morganna scoffed. "Since when do I ever sleep?"

A soft huff of laughter escaped him, the sound oddly comforting in the vast emptiness of the night. "Fair point."

The terraces were empty at this hour—just the way she liked them. No watching eyes. No expectations pressing down on her shoulders like invisible chains. Just stone beneath her boots, stars above her head, and the constant pulse of magic woven into her bones.

She stretched her arms above her head, rolling out her shoulders, shaking off the tension she hadn't realized was coiled tight beneath her skin. Then she glanced at Aeron, flashing him a grin sharp enough to cut through the lingering weight between them.

"Spar with me."

His brow arched, a shadow of amusement flickering in his storm-gray eyes. "You want to fight now?"

"Unless you're afraid."

That did it.

A slow, dangerous smirk tugged at the corner of his mouth. "I'm never afraid of you, Morganna."

She liked the way he said her name—grounded, without the weight of titles or expectations. Just her.

Without warning, she lunged.

Aeron dodged easily, stepping aside with infuriating grace, his hand shooting out to catch her wrist mid-strike. His fingers closed around her like iron wrapped in velvet—strong, unyielding, but careful.

Morganna spun with the momentum, twisting out of his grip, her foot sliding against the smooth stone as she shifted her stance. A wicked grin pulled at her lips, heart racing—not from fear, but from the sheer exhilaration of movement, of freedom, of *this*.

They moved like echoes of themselves—two sides of the same coin, perfectly balanced between precision and chaos. Their bodies knew this dance better than their minds did: a rhythm carved from years of training, sparring, surviving.

Magic pulsed beneath their skin, crackling at the edges, restrained but ready to spill over if either of them slipped.

Morganna ducked under a quick strike, laughter bubbling out—real, breathless, and unguarded. She hadn't realized how much she needed this. To move. To feel. To be more than just the girl carrying the weight of a fraying destiny.

Aeron's grin was sharp as he lunged again, faster this time. She twisted, dodging—*almost*.

His leg hooked behind hers, and before she could recover, she hit the ground with a hard thud, the breath rushing out of her lungs.

Before she could react, he was on top of her, pinning her wrists against the cool stone.

Morganna's breath caught. Not from the fall. Not from the fight. But because of *him*.

They were both breathing hard, chests rising and falling in a rhythm that felt too synchronized to be accidental. His face was inches from hers, his storm-gray eyes dark and unreadable, shadows dancing across his sharp features in the starlight.

His grip on her wrists wasn't rough. It wasn't even tight. Just… steady. Like he was holding on not because he needed to—but because he *wanted* to.

Her pulse pounded in her ears, drowning out everything except the faint hum of his magic—subtle, like static before a storm. His fingers flexed slightly, the movement small but enough to send a shiver racing up her arms.

And suddenly, she wasn't thinking about the fight anymore. She wasn't thinking about the Weave. Or the Council. Or the unraveling threads of fate that had been slipping through her fingers like sand.

She was thinking about *him*.

His gaze flicked downward—just for a second. Barely there. She felt it like a lightning strike.

Dangerous.

She should've pushed him off. Said something sharp and dismissive. Deflect, distract, deny. It was the Guardian way. It was *their* way.

But she didn't move. Neither did he.

The stars burned cold and bright above them, silent witnesses to a moment carved from everything they weren't allowed to feel.

Then—like a breath being held too long—Aeron exhaled sharply and let go.

The moment snapped, fragile as glass.

He pushed himself up, offering a hand to help her to her feet, his expression carefully blank.

Morganna hesitated for half a second, then took it, ignoring the way her skin still tingled where his fingers had been.

They didn't speak about it. They never did.

Instead, she dusted herself off, forcing a smirk onto her face like armor. "Lucky shot."

Aeron gave her a look, one brow arched with infuriating smugness. "If you say so."

***

Later, they sat at the edge of the terrace, legs dangling over the abyss below. The stone was cool beneath them, the wind sharp against their skin, carrying with it the faint hum of the Weave—a sound so constant it was easy to forget it was there.

But not tonight. Tonight, it felt louder.

Morganna pulled her knees to her chest, resting her chin against them. The stars above seemed dimmer, like the universe itself was tired.

"We need to figure out what's happening," she said quietly, her voice sounding too small against the vastness around them.

Aeron nodded, his gaze distant, locked on the horizon where the sky bled into shadow. "I know."

She turned to look at him. "If the Council won't help, that means we're on our own."

His jaw tightened slightly, but he didn't argue. "Where do we start?"

Morganna considered for a moment, her mind tracing invisible threads, trying to find the right knot to pull. "The Heartstone."

Aeron exhaled through his nose, the sound almost a laugh but not quite. "I was afraid you'd say that."

She nudged him with her shoulder, a faint smile tugging at the corner of her mouth. "You say that like we haven't broken into the archives before."

He glanced at her, his lips quirking. "We were younger. That was different."

"Was it?"

A beat of silence stretched between them.

Then Aeron sighed, shaking his head. "No. It really wasn't."

She grinned. "Exactly."

There was something easy about this—about *them*. The way they could plot treason like it was a game, the way they fit together without needing to explain the pieces.

Morganna's smile faded as her thoughts drifted back to the fragile threads of the Weave. "The Heartstone's magic is older than the Guardians. If something is shifting, it has to be recorded there."

Aeron's smirk faded, his expression turning serious again. "And if it's worse than we think?"

The question hung in the air, sharp as a blade.

If the Council was covering this up, it wasn't just politics or pride. It meant the unraveling wasn't some isolated ripple.

It was a fracture.

Morganna turned her gaze back to the stars. They'd always felt like an anchor—constant, distant, eternal. Tonight, they flickered.

She exhaled slowly. "Then we find a way to fix it."

Aeron didn't respond right away. His silence stretched just long enough to make her wonder if he was going to say something he shouldn't.

Then, finally, he spoke.

"You always act like fate is something you can fix."

She glanced at him, her brow arching. "Because it is."

His eyes met hers, storm-gray and steady. "What if it's not?"

Morganna didn't answer.

Because for the first time in her life, she wasn't sure if he was wrong.

Chapter 4

"The truth is like a thread pulled from a tapestry—once it begins to unravel, you can never weave it back the same way again."

The halls of the Citadel were silent at this hour.

Not truly empty—there were always wardens, always eyes hidden behind enchanted barriers—but silent enough. The kind of silence that made Morganna's pulse race, turning every footstep into a potential betrayal. The polished stone beneath her boots seemed too loud, the faint hum of the Weave too sharp, like the Citadel itself was holding its breath, waiting for them to make a mistake.

Aeron moved beside her, quiet as ever, his steps a shadow to her own. His magic pulsed beneath the surface—not overt, but there—like static in the air before a storm. If they were caught, he'd be the one to talk them out of it. That was the unspoken rule between them.

Morganna caused the trouble. Aeron made sure they survived it.

They navigated the labyrinthine corridors with the ease of familiarity, passing towering arches etched with runes that shimmered faintly in the dim glow of the crystal sconces lining the walls. The air grew colder as they descended, the magic woven into the very stone thickening with each step.

At last, they reached the outer doors of the High Archives.

The towering obsidian gates loomed before them, carved with ancient symbols that seemed to writhe and shift when viewed from the corner of the eye. Protective runes glowed faintly across the surface—lines of silver and gold threaded like veins beneath black stone. These were no simple wards. This was the history of fate itself, locked behind magic older than most Guardians could comprehend.

Only a handful of Guardians were allowed entry. They were not among them.

Morganna smirked, rolling her shoulders and flexing her fingers as her magic stirred beneath her skin, eager and reckless. "Good thing we don't care about rules."

Aeron shot her a look, his mouth tugging into the faintest smirk. "You mean *you* don't."

She grinned, stepping forward and placing her palms lightly against the cold stone. The runes pulsed beneath her touch, like a heartbeat just under the surface. She closed her eyes, letting her magic seep into the structure, reaching for the threads woven into the wards.

Everything had a thread. And everything could be unwoven.

She found them easily enough—delicate strands woven with precision, layered upon layers of enchantments designed to deter, to resist. She traced them with her mind, searching for the weak points, the knots hidden beneath the patterns.

The runes flared beneath her touch, a sharp pulse of static crackling through the air.

Aeron tensed beside her. "Morganna—"

"Relax," she whispered, feeling the pattern shift under her careful manipulation. She nudged at the threads, teasing them apart with the precision of a blade sliding between ribs. "I've got it."

Another pulse. But this time, it wasn't just a flare.

The Weave shivered around her fingers, like something alive—like it felt her there—and it *pushed back.*

Morganna's breath caught. Resisting?

Magic had never fought her before. Not like this.

For a fraction of a second, she hesitated. And in that second, the Weave retaliated.

A shockwave of energy surged through the air, slamming into her chest with the force of a hammer. She staggered backward, her vision flashing white as pain exploded across her ribs. She would've hit the cold stone floor if Aeron hadn't caught her, his arms strong and steady around her, grounding her as the magic's echoes faded.

"Morganna," he breathed, his voice sharp, urgent, threaded with something else—something too close to fear.

She gritted her teeth, forcing her legs to hold her weight, though they trembled beneath her. "I'm fine."

He didn't let go immediately. His grip lingered, fingers firm around her arms, his magic humming faintly against her skin. Steady. Grounding. *Too* close.

She inhaled, her hands splayed against his chest, feeling the rapid, steady thrum of his heartbeat beneath her palms. The warmth of him bled through the thin fabric of his tunic, anchoring her more effectively than any spell.

Then, with a controlled breath, he released her. The absence of his touch felt colder than the stone walls.

She stepped back, shaking off the lingering buzz of the backlash, swallowing the tight knot in her throat. "Okay. That was... different."

"Different?" His voice was low, edged with frustration. "It just threw you across the hall, Morganna. That's not *different*—that's *dangerous.*"

She dragged a hand through her hair, still feeling the static crackling at her fingertips. "The Weave's never done that before."

Aeron's jaw clenched, the muscle ticking as he stared at the runes. "Because the Weave has never been broken before."

The words hit harder than the shockwave had. They hung between them, heavy and undeniable.

Morganna turned back to the door, studying the threads more carefully this time. The magic wasn't just resisting.

It was *fraying*.

Unraveling from the inside out, like a tapestry rotting beneath its surface—its patterns still intact, but hollow.

And that terrified her.

Because if even fate's own defenses were starting to unravel... Then maybe the Council already knew. Maybe they were already too late.

She exhaled sharply, pushing the thought aside. "We still need to get inside."

Aeron crossed his arms over his chest, his expression dark. "And if the next attempt hurls you into a different realm?"

She flashed him a grin, though it felt thin around the edges. "Then you'll have to come save me."

He didn't smile. He just watched her, eyes too steady, too quiet—like he was seeing past the bravado, past the grin, straight into the fear she couldn't admit.

Morganna sighed, rubbing the heel of her palm against her temple. "Fine. Plan B."

Aeron arched a brow. "You have a Plan B?"

She gave him an exaggerated look of offense. "I *always* have a Plan B."

Reaching into her pocket, she pulled out a small braided charm. It was simple, barely the size of a coin, woven with faint strands of magic that glimmered softly in the dim corridor light.

Aeron's expression shifted the moment he saw it. His guarded mask slipped just enough for her to catch the flicker of recognition in his eyes.

"That's—"

"You remember this, don't you?" she murmured, turning the charm over between her fingers. The silver thread gleamed faintly, warm against her skin.

He was quiet for a moment. Then, softly: "Yeah."

Because he was the one who had given it to her. Years ago. Back when she was still new to the Guardians, still stumbling under the weight of expectations she wasn't sure she could meet. Back when she'd sat alone in the Archives, exhausted and frustrated, her magic raw and untamed, convinced she didn't belong.

And Aeron—damn him—had found her there. Without judgment. Without pity.

He'd handed her this. A simple silver-threaded charm, small enough to tie around her wrist.

For luck, he'd said. *For when you need a little extra balance.*

It had been nothing. It had been everything.

Now, she pressed it against the runes etched into the obsidian gates.

And this time, the magic yielded.

The runes pulsed softly, the harsh resistance fading as the threads of enchantment loosened beneath her touch. A soft click echoed through the corridor as the ancient wards disengaged, the doors groaning as they unlocked for the first time in centuries.

Aeron exhaled, the sound barely audible. "You never told me you kept it."

Morganna didn't look at him. Didn't dare. "Of course I did."

Another heartbeat of silence stretched between them, fragile and full of all the things they never said.

Then the gates creaked open, revealing the endless halls of the High Archives beyond—rows upon rows of ancient texts, enchanted tomes, and relics glowing faintly in the darkness. The air was colder here, thick with magic, with secrets woven into every stone.

Morganna stepped inside first, her pulse steady even as her thoughts tangled in ways she couldn't control. Behind her, Aeron lingered just a moment longer. Then he followed. Because he always did.

***

The High Archives were too quiet.

Morganna had expected something—an enchanted ward flaring to life, a spectral guardian, even a stern-faced archivist hunched over dusty tomes. But the vast halls stretched out before them, shelves upon shelves of ancient texts, stone tablets, and scrolls wrapped in brittle parchment, bathed in the eerie, flickering glow of enchanted lanterns suspended from vaulted ceilings.

The silence wasn't peaceful. It was the kind that pressed against her ears, thick and suffocating, like the very walls were holding their breath.

Her gut twisted.

Something wasn't right.

Aeron felt it too. His steps grew quieter, more deliberate, his hand resting lightly on the hilt of the dagger strapped to his belt. She could feel the faint pulse of his magic humming beneath his skin, restrained but ready—like a storm waiting just beyond the horizon.

Morganna didn't waste time. They weren't supposed to be here, and if the Weave itself had already tried to stop them, there was no telling what—or *who*—might intervene next.

She moved quickly, her fingers trailing over the spines of ancient books, each one embossed with symbols older than memory. The dust clinging to the shelves was undisturbed, untouched for what felt like centuries, and the faint scent of parchment and ink mixed with something faintly metallic—like blood long since dried.

The Fractured Thread Prophecy. It echoed in her mind, sharp and unrelenting.

Aeron scanned the shelves beside her, his eyes flicking over titles in languages long dead. "You think this is about the prophecy?"

"I don't know," she muttered, frustration curling tight in her chest. "But if the Weave is breaking and the Council refuses to talk about it, that means they're hiding something."

Aeron didn't argue. He never did when she was right.

They worked fast, pulling texts, scanning them, discarding anything irrelevant. Dust stirred in the stale air with every movement, catching the dim light like ash floating in the aftermath of a fire. The flickering lanterns cast long, shifting shadows across the marble floor—shadows that seemed to move just a little too much when she wasn't looking directly at them.

Her pulse quickened.

Then— She froze.

Her fingers brushed over a book that felt *wrong*. Not cold. Not warm. Just... *off.* Like it didn't belong. Like it shouldn't exist.

She pulled it free from the shelf, the leather-bound cover cool and smooth despite the layers of dust coating it. The symbol etched into the spine—a circle bisected by a jagged line—seemed to shimmer faintly as her magic brushed against it.

She flipped it open.

The pages were brittle, the ink faded with time, written in a script that shifted slightly when she tried to focus on it. But the words burned themselves into her mind.

"When love defies where fate decrees, A golden thread shall come undone. The Heart will break, the heavens mourn, And darkness' reign will have begun.

Born of light yet bound to Weave, A child too bright, too wild to chain. She holds the key to all that is— Yet love will set the world aflame.

A choice will come, a cost in blood, A tether lost to time's cruel hand. Should shadow claim a heart once pure, Then love itself will curse the land.

But echoes stir within the dark, A severed thread still sings its song. Twelve shall rise to heal the past, And weave anew what love made wrong."

Morganna's stomach dropped.

Aeron appeared at her side, peering over her shoulder. "That's not cryptic at all," he muttered dryly.

Morganna ignored him, her heart pounding as she flipped through the fragile pages, faster now, desperate for more. There had to be more—something that explained why the Weave was failing *now*.

Then she saw it.

A single line, scrawled in the margin. A note written hastily, the ink darker and fresher than the rest, though it had to be ancient.

The Weave does not break. It is unwoven. And the one who wields the Heartstone—

The ink ended abruptly. Like the writer had been interrupted. Or worse.

Morganna's pulse roared in her ears.

Aeron's hand landed on her shoulder, firm and grounding. "Morganna."

She barely heard him. Because the air around them had shifted.

The flickering lanterns sputtered once—then snuffed out, plunging the room into darkness.

A gust of wind—impossible, unnatural—ripped through the chamber, scattering loose papers like leaves in a storm. The shelves groaned as if the weight of their knowledge was suddenly too much to bear, and the floor beneath their feet trembled, just for a heartbeat, like the Citadel itself was rejecting their presence.

Aeron's grip tightened. "We need to go. Now."

Morganna didn't argue. She snapped the book shut, tucking it into her belt as they bolted, the echo of their footsteps swallowed by the oppressive darkness.

The shelves blurred past them, walls closing in, shadows twisting unnaturally at the edges of her vision—stretching, reaching, like fingers clawing at the corners of reality.

Then— The door they'd come through slammed shut with a deafening boom, the sound vibrating through her chest.

Morganna skidded to a stop, Aeron right behind her. She thrust out her hand, magic sparking at her fingertips— But the door was *gone*.

Not locked. Not sealed. *Gone.*

Replaced by endless black stone, smooth and unbroken where an entrance had been moments before.

Her breath caught. "That's... not good."

Aeron turned slowly, his dagger now drawn, the blade catching what little ambient light remained. "I was hoping for 'mildly inconvenient,' but sure, let's go with 'not good.'"

The air grew thick, heavy like water, pressing against her chest, making it hard to breathe. Morganna reached for the Weave, desperate to grasp its familiar threads, to bend them, break them, *escape*—

Pain lanced through her skull like a spike driven straight into her mind.

She staggered, collapsing to one knee, clutching her head as searing white light burned behind her eyes. Her magic recoiled, slipping through her fingers like smoke.

Something—*someone*—was inside the Weave. Watching. Waiting. *Hunting.*

"Morganna!"

Aeron's voice felt distant, distorted, like it was echoing from the other side of a chasm. She barely registered his hands gripping her arms, shaking her, his touch the only thing anchoring her to reality.

But even that anchor wasn't enough.

A whisper slithered through the darkness, soft and venomous, curling around her mind.

"You shouldn't have come here."

Morganna gasped as the world tilted violently sideways. A flash of gold. A sound like glass shattering underwater. A scream—maybe hers, maybe not.

And then— Nothing.

The Void

Morganna hit the ground hard.

The impact knocked the breath from her lungs, her body jolting against the unyielding surface as stone bit into her hands and knees. Pain flared up her spine, sharp and disorienting, but it was nothing compared to the overwhelming *wrongness* that followed.

The world spun around her, her vision blurring into streaks of shattered gold and unraveling threads, as if reality itself couldn't decide how to hold together.

Aeron landed beside her in a crouch, his instincts sharp even now. He was already upright, his movements fluid and controlled, his hand twitching toward the dagger at his belt. His magic pulsed beneath the surface—steady, like the faint drumbeat of a war he was always ready to fight.

But there was no enemy to face.

Because the archives were *gone*.

No towering shelves, no ancient tomes, no flickering lanterns. Just... *nothing*.

An endless expanse of void stretched out around them in every direction—a vast, oppressive emptiness that felt deeper than space itself. No walls, no ceiling, no ground, even though they were somehow standing. It was as if they were suspended within a place that had been erased from existence.

Morganna swallowed hard, her heart pounding against her ribs.

"That's... new," Aeron muttered, his voice low, the humor brittle at the edges.

She forced herself to her feet, dusting off her cloak with a flick that felt more like defiance than necessity. "Understatement of the century."

But the air—the air felt *wrong*. Heavy. Stagnant. Thick like oil, pressing against her chest, making it hard to breathe. It wasn't just the absence of walls. It was the absence of *everything*.

And worse— She couldn't feel the Weave.

Morganna's breath hitched. Panic prickled at the edges of her mind, sharp and sudden. She reached for it instinctively, stretching her senses outward, seeking the familiar hum of fate's threads that had always been there.

Nothing.

Not a flicker. Not a whisper. Just... *void.*

Her heart stuttered. She spun toward Aeron, her pulse hammering in her throat. "I—I can't touch it."

Aeron's expression shifted instantly. His eyes sharpened, cutting through the dim, featureless expanse around them to lock onto hers. "What do you mean?"

"The Weave. It's—" She pressed a hand to her chest, right over her heart, where her magic usually thrummed in perfect rhythm with the world. "It's not here. It's like I've been *cut off.*"

A muscle in Aeron's jaw twitched. "That shouldn't be possible."

"No. It shouldn't."

And yet... here they were.

Morganna clenched her fists, trying to steady her breathing, even as her magic screamed silently in the void—empty, like someone had reached inside her and torn out a piece of her soul. She had always been connected to the Weave. It wasn't just part of her—it *was* her. The idea of being severed from it...

It was like drowning without water.

She shook her head sharply. *No. Focus.* Panic wouldn't get them out of here.

Aeron pivoted, his stance tense, scanning the endless nothing. His body was taut with readiness, every muscle coiled for a fight that had no visible enemy. "There has to be a way out."

Morganna let out a sharp, bitter laugh. "It's not like there's a door, Aeron."

"We didn't walk in through a door, either."

Fair point.

She looked around again, her frustration mounting with every breath. She didn't get trapped. She didn't get caught. She was Morganna, Guardian of Balance—Weaveborn. But none of that seemed to matter here.

Something had brought them here. Which meant something was watching.

***

Aeron stepped closer, his presence grounding her like it always did. "If we're cut off from the Weave, we need to think outside of it."

She shot him a wary glance. "Meaning?"

He hesitated—just for a second, which was rare for him. Like he wasn't sure she'd like the answer. Then—carefully—he reached out, his fingers wrapping around her wrist.

The moment his skin touched hers, everything changed.

Magic surged through her veins, fierce and wild, like a lightning strike with no place to land. Morganna gasped, her spine arching as the shockwave rippled through her, leaving every nerve ending raw and burning.

Not the Weave. Something else. Something older. *Him.*

Aeron's magic. Not bound to fate, not part of the tapestry she had always known. His power came from the Aether—raw, unfiltered energy, drawn from the very spaces between the threads of reality.

And right now? It was the only thing keeping her from disappearing entirely.

Aeron's grip tightened, his eyes darkening with concern. "What are you feeling?"

She struggled to catch her breath, her heart slamming against her ribs like it was trying to escape. "I—I don't know. It's—" *Him.* She could feel him—not just his magic, but everything. The steady thrum of his heartbeat, the warmth of his skin, the sharp focus of his mind. Their magic tangled together, not neatly woven, but colliding like wildfire against stone.

"Aeron," she gasped. "I think— I think your magic is still working."

Aeron frowned, his jaw tightening. "That doesn't make sense."

"I know." She swallowed hard. "But it's the only thing keeping me from—"

A cold whisper curled through the void, soft and slick like oil sliding over glass.

"You don't belong here."

Morganna and Aeron reacted simultaneously, breaking apart with practiced precision, weapons drawn. Her dagger flashed with residual golden light, while his blade shimmered faintly with Aetheric energy, sharp and humming like it hungered for release.

A shadow coalesced before them.

Not a figure. Not truly. Just... an absence of light, twisting unnaturally, darker than the void around it. No face. No eyes. Just a shape formed from nothingness, its edges flickering like static.

The darkness wasn't empty. It was *hungry.*

Aeron shifted instinctively, positioning himself between Morganna and the shadow, his magic crackling at his fingertips, fierce and volatile. "Who are you?"

The shadow laughed.

A low, guttural sound, more like the *idea* of laughter than the real thing. It echoed inside Morganna's skull, vibrating through her bones.

"You shouldn't have come here, little Guardian."

A sickening pulse ripped through the space, and Morganna staggered, clutching her chest as another shockwave of magic slammed into her, sending sparks of white-hot pain through her ribs.

The same feeling she'd had when the Weave pushed back.

Her stomach dropped.

"You," she whispered, her voice rough with disbelief and fury. *"You're the reason the Weave is unraveling."*

The shadow shifted—subtle, fluid, like smoke caught in an invisible wind. No denial. No confirmation. Just silence.

Then—without warning—it lunged.

A mass of black tendrils exploded from its form, whipping toward them like blades.

Aeron moved first.

He yanked Morganna behind him, thrusting his hand forward as a barrier of pure Aetheric energy erupted between them and the oncoming attack. The tendrils struck the shield with a force that sent shockwaves through the void, sparks of raw magic cascading like shattered glass.

Morganna didn't wait.

She pushed past the fear, past the pain, and reached for the tangled remnants of her power—Aeron's magic still woven into hers like threads pulled too tight.

She threw everything she had left into one desperate strike.

A pulse of golden light burst from her palms, slamming into the shadow with enough force to make the void itself tremble.

The entity *screamed*.

Not in pain. In rage.

The sound was unbearable—like glass shattering inside her skull, like reality itself was fracturing at the seams.

The void cracked.

Morganna felt it—the world pulling apart, collapsing in on itself, a sensation of falling without moving, like every thread of reality was snapping at once.

The shadow surged toward her, faster than thought, faster than fear.

Aeron grabbed her hand.

"Morganna—*hold on!*"

And then— The world collapsed.

***

The void did not release them gently.

One moment, they were drowning in endless black, the silence pressing into their lungs, their souls unraveling thread by fragile thread. The next—

Light.

Morganna gasped, her body collapsing onto the stone floor of the Archives, the ancient air thick and stifling compared to the cold emptiness of the void. Her fingers twitched, instinctively searching—

Aeron.

She felt his presence before she saw him, his hand gripping hers with a desperation that mirrored her own. His breathing was ragged, his body tense as if he expected the void to claw him back at any moment.

She turned her head, finding his gaze—wild, uncertain. His grip on her tightened, grounding them both.

"You're here," he murmured, almost as if he was testing the words, as if speaking them made it real.

Morganna swallowed hard, nodding. The void still echoed inside her, a whisper clinging to the edges of her mind, a darkness that hadn't quite let go.

But they were back.

And that was all that mattered.

"Morganna."

Aeron's voice—rough, strained, but there.

She turned her head, relief crashing over her like a wave. Aeron was beside her, pushing himself up on one arm, his face tense with effort. His tunic was torn at the shoulder, streaks of dried blood staining the fabric, and his breathing was uneven, shallow.

Her chest clenched. "Are you hurt?"

He shook his head, though the movement was tight with pain. "I'm fine. You?"

She flexed her fingers. Her magic was distant, like a faint echo at the edge of her senses, stretched thin and frayed—but at least it was there. She could feel it again.

"I'll live," she rasped.

Aeron let out a breath of relief, his posture softening just enough to betray how tense he'd been. But there was no time to linger in that fragile moment.

His eyes swept the room, sharp and assessing. "What the hell was that?"

Morganna swallowed hard, her throat dry. The truth felt like glass in her mouth.

"That thing... it wasn't just feeding on the Weave." She forced herself to her feet, her legs trembling beneath her. "It was *breaking* it."

Aeron's jaw clenched, the muscle ticking as his eyes darkened. "And the Council just... let it happen?"

Morganna thought of the Oracle. The lie in his voice. The way the High Guardians had dismissed her warnings like she was a child chasing shadows.

No. They hadn't ignored the unraveling. They'd *known*.

And they'd chosen silence.

Her rage burned hot and fast, but she shoved it down. No time for fury—not yet.

She reached for Aeron, helping him to his feet. "We need to get out of here. Now."

He nodded grimly. "Agreed."

But just as they turned toward the exit—

The library doors exploded open.

Morganna's stomach plummeted.

A dozen figures flooded into the Archives, their footsteps a synchronized echo of authority and violence. Cloaks embroidered with silver-threaded sigils snapped like banners in the rush of air, the insignia of the Guardian Wardens—elite enforcers of the Citadel.

Shit.

Aeron's hand shot out, gripping her wrist, his body instinctively shifting to shield her even though they were hopelessly outnumbered.

The lead Warden stepped forward, his face obscured by the dark hood of his cloak, but the authority in his voice was unmistakable—sharp as steel, cold as ice.

"Guardians Morganna and Aeron," he announced, his words echoing off the stone walls. "You are under arrest for unauthorized entry into the High Archives."

Morganna didn't flinch. Didn't blink. She just smiled—sharp and defiant.

"You're going to wish that was all we did."

Chapter 5

"Chains may hold the body, but they cannot hold the will. And the will, once set free, is the most dangerous thing of all."

Magic surged through the air before Morganna could react—fast, brutal, and cold as winter steel.

The wardens weren't ordinary Guardians. Their power was tethered directly to the Heartstone, making them stronger, faster, more precise—impossible to outrun. Their movements were almost mechanical, as if fate itself guided their blades.

She tried to move, tried to summon her magic, but golden bindings snapped around her wrists with a hiss like molten metal meeting ice. A searing pulse shot through her veins, severing her connection to the Weave. The sudden absence was like being plunged underwater with no chance to breathe—her magic slipping through her fingers like drowning in plain air. She clenched her fists, expecting a flicker of golden light. Nothing. Just empty air. The void where her magic should be felt worse than pain—it felt like being erased. She had been connected to the weave and her magic her entire life.

Across the room, Aeron roared, his voice raw with fury. He lashed out with a burst of raw Aetheric energy, brilliant and blinding—but three wardens surged forward, their enchanted blades cutting through the burst like it was nothing more than smoke. They overwhelmed him with ruthless efficiency, moving as one, relentless and cold. Aeron fought like a cornered wolf—wild, teeth bared, refusing to go down without a fight. But the enchanted restraints coiled around him, crackling with magic that forced him to his knees with a brutal thud.

One of the wardens saw her reaction to the loss of magic, and told her "Get used to it, you won't be needing your magic where you're going."

Morganna's heart pounded, her breath coming in sharp, shallow gasps. *No. This isn't how it's supposed to end.*

They had been so close.

The prophecy. The unraveling. The truth—it was right there, within reach.

And now? Now, they were prisoners.

She twisted against the bindings, her wrists burning where the metal bit into her skin, the faint scent of scorched flesh filling her nose. "You don't understand—"

"I understand perfectly," the lead warden snapped, stepping closer.

His face came into view—harsh jawline, eyes like chips of obsidian, devoid of empathy. His voice was as sharp as the blade strapped to his side, each word cutting deeper than the last.

"You violated direct orders from the High Council. You trespassed in restricted archives. You will answer for your crimes."

Crimes.

Morganna clenched her fists, the bindings digging deeper, drawing thin lines of blood. *What about the real crime?*

What about the fact that the Weave was breaking? That something was tearing fate apart at its seams while the Council sat on their thrones and did nothing?

Her rage surged, hot and blinding, but Aeron's eyes caught hers—a subtle shake of his head. *Not here. Not now.*

She swallowed the fury burning in her throat, her jaw aching from the effort. They were outnumbered. Outpowered. And if they were going to survive—if they were going to fix this—they needed another plan. Fast.

***

The prison beneath the Citadel was as old as the Guardians themselves.

Carved deep into the bedrock, it was a place untouched by time—cold, oppressive, and utterly devoid of hope. The walls were etched with ancient runes that pulsed faintly, their sickly glow casting jagged shadows. They weren't just decorative. They were designed to suppress magic, to sever any connection to the Weave.

Morganna sat on a stone bench, her wrists still bound in enchanted chains. The cold metal bit into her skin, leeching away what little warmth she had left. The faint hum of the suppression runes thrummed in her ears, a relentless reminder of her powerlessness. Her magic felt distant, like a phantom limb—there, but useless. It was like losing a piece of herself, like trying to breathe with no air.

Across the cell, Aeron leaned against the opposite wall, arms crossed over his chest. Despite the bruises blooming across his skin and the blood staining his sleeve, he looked infuriatingly calm. His storm-gray eyes were unreadable, distant, as if this was nothing more than an inconvenience. But Morganna knew better.

"Tell me you have a plan," she muttered, her voice low and hoarse with frustration.

Aeron tilted his head slightly, a faint smirk tugging at the corner of his mouth. "Do I ever *not* have a plan?"

Despite herself, she snorted—a sharp, breathless sound that tasted like defiance.

She exhaled, her fingers curling around the cold metal of her restraints. The bite of iron against her skin grounded her, a small reminder that she was still here, still fighting. "They're not going to let us out of here. The Council wants this buried."

"I know."

She turned her gaze on him, really looked at him—the sharp angles of his face, the shadows carved beneath his eyes, the quiet strength in his posture. The way he always, *always* chose to stand beside her. Even now. Even when it meant going against everything they'd sworn to protect.

Her heart ached with something sharp and dangerous.

They couldn't stay here. If they did, the unraveling would continue. The Weave would collapse. And if the High Guardians refused to stop it...

Then she would. With or without them.

Morganna took a slow breath, her voice steady despite the storm raging inside her. "We need to escape."

Aeron didn't hesitate. "I know."

His certainty sent a shiver through her—because there had never been a question. Because he had never once doubted her. Because Aeron was hers. And he would follow her anywhere.

She shifted closer, lowering her voice to a whisper. "We don't have much time. They'll put us on trial, make an example of us. We need to get to the Heartstone before that happens."

Aeron's expression darkened, his jaw tightening. "They'll never let us near it."

"Not willingly."

Silence stretched between them, thick with unspoken words. Then—slowly—Aeron's mouth curled into a familiar, dangerous smirk.

"That's why we won't ask."

Her pulse skipped. *Gods, she loved him.* She shouldn't. She couldn't. But she did.

And if fate thought it could tear him away from her— It had another thing coming.

***

Morganna hated waiting.

The cold stone floor beneath her boots felt like it was mocking her—solid, unyielding, just like the enchanted chains biting into her wrists. She paced the narrow length of the holding cell, her breath shallow with frustration. Every second that passed was another thread slipping loose from the Weave. Another second lost.

Across the cell, Aeron leaned against the wall like he had all the time in the world. Arms crossed. Relaxed. Too relaxed. His face was the picture of calm, but Morganna knew him too well. Beneath the stillness was tension coiled like a blade, sharp and ready.

It drove her insane.

She spun on him, her voice low and sharp. "How are you just standing there?"

Aeron tilted his head slightly, the corner of his mouth twitching into a familiar, infuriating smirk. "Because I know something you don't."

Her eyes narrowed. "Aeron—"

The torches lining the corridor outside their cell flickered. Once. Twice.

Then darkness swallowed the hallway, as if the light itself had been snuffed out—not just dimmed, but *erased*.

Silence.

A low, distant rumble vibrated through the floor beneath her feet. Then— *BOOM*.

The prison shook with the force of an explosion. Dust rained down from the ceiling, and Morganna's pulse spiked.

She whipped around, eyes darting toward the reinforced metal door at the end of the hall.

"Aeron," she hissed, heart pounding. "*What the hell did you do?*"

Aeron casually pushed off the wall, rolling his shoulders like he was warming up for a fight. "Nothing." His grin widened. "*Yet.*"

Before she could respond, the heavy door burst open, slamming into the stone wall with enough force to rattle the iron bars of their cell.

A Guardian stumbled into view—then crumpled to the ground, unconscious.

Morganna's heart lurched, but she barely had time to process before a shadow filled the doorway.

A hooded figure stepped into the flickering half-light, dust swirling around him like mist. A sharp grin flashed beneath the shadow of his hood. A glint of silver at his belt.

No.

"Did you miss me?"

Morganna's stomach dropped.

"*Rhylen?*"

Aeron groaned, dragging a hand down his face. "Of course it's Rhylen."

The rogue Guardian winked, sauntering forward with all the reckless swagger Morganna remembered—and hated. "I was in the neighborhood."

Rhylen was never *in the neighborhood.*

Morganna opened her mouth to demand an explanation, but Rhylen was already in motion. He tossed something through the bars with lazy precision.

Aeron caught it midair—a small blade, simple and lethal, forged with dark metal etched in faint runes.

Before Morganna could blink, Aeron moved.

The chains snapped with a sharp *crack,* the magic woven into them dissolving like smoke. Morganna's magic surged back into her veins in an instant, fierce and overwhelming, like a dam breaking.

She didn't hesitate.

A pulse of golden light erupted from her palms, slamming into the cell door.

The iron exploded outward in a shower of molten metal and fractured stone.

Rhylen let out a low whistle from where he lounged against the opposite wall, completely unfazed by the destruction. "*I did miss you.*"

Morganna ignored him. No time. No distractions.

She turned to Aeron, her magic still sparking at her fingertips. "We need to move."

Aeron nodded, tossing the broken shackles aside. "Where to?"

"The Heartstone," she said without hesitation. "We need to see it for ourselves."

Aeron exhaled sharply. "That's the most heavily guarded part of the Citadel."

Morganna flashed him a wicked grin. "Then we better move fast."

Aeron's lips twitched, the faintest hint of a smile ghosting across his face. *Gods, he loved her like this—fierce, reckless, unstoppable.*

Rhylen sighed dramatically, dusting off his cloak. "Oh good. A suicide mission. I was getting bored."

Morganna didn't wait for more sarcasm. She ran.

Aeron and Rhylen followed.

Chapter 6

"Fate may chase us, chains may bind us, but as long as we run, we are not yet caught." They moved fast.

The lower levels of the Citadel were a labyrinth of narrow stone corridors and spiraling staircases, the walls slick with condensation and etched with ancient runes meant to keep prisoners in, not to keep intruders out. That gave them an advantage.

But not for long.

The alarm bells began to ring—a piercing, metallic sound that echoed off the stone like the Citadel itself was screaming. The vibrations hummed through the walls, growing louder with every heartbeat. The Guardians were awake now, and the hunt had begun.

Morganna's heart raced in time with her footsteps, adrenaline burning through her veins like wildfire. She skidded to a stop at an intersection, boots slipping slightly on the damp floor. The air smelled of stone dust and old magic.

Boots thundered behind them—closer now.

Aeron's voice was sharp, breathless. "Left or right?"

She scanned the maze of hallways.

Left led deeper into the prison—dead end.

Right opened into the outer courtyard—wide, exposed, no cover. Dangerous. But possible.

"Right!" Morganna snapped, already sprinting.

Aeron didn't question her. He never did. Rhylen groaned as he ran. "Why is it always the dangerous option with you?" "Because I'm always right," she shot back.

***

They burst into the open, the sudden expanse of space jarring after the tight corridors.

The courtyard stretched wide beneath the night sky, moonlight glinting off slick stone polished by years of footsteps. Rain hung in the air like mist, making everything shimmer. Cracked statues of long-forgotten Guardians loomed at the edges, their faces eroded by time.

But Morganna's relief was short-lived.

Her stomach dropped.

A battalion of Guardians stood waiting.

At least twenty of them, armored in gleaming silver, their weapons glowing with runes etched deep into the metal—halberds, swords, staffs crackling with raw power. Their formation was tight, disciplined, cutting off every possible exit. Their faces were hidden behind visors, but she could feel the weight of their collective focus like a blade pressed to her throat.

Rhylen skidded to a stop beside her, panting. "Well," he breathed, "this is awkward."

Morganna clenched her fists, her magic pulsing just beneath her skin like it wanted to break free. She refused to stop now. She refused to be caged again.

Aeron stepped up beside her, his face calm, his gray eyes burning with quiet fury. The Aether around him crackled like static, the air vibrating with restrained power.

Outnumbered. Outpowered. But not out of options.

Morganna's smirk was razor-sharp. "How do you feel about breaking more rules?" Aeron's jaw tightened. His eyes met hers. "Always."

***

The first bolt of magic came fast—too fast.

Morganna barely twisted out of the way as a spear of golden energy tore through the air, slamming into the stone where she'd stood a heartbeat earlier. The ground exploded in a flash of heat and shattered rock, debris pelting her like shrapnel.

Aeron moved instantly.

He yanked her back just as a second blast streaked toward them. His arm locked around her waist, anchoring her, while his free hand lashed out. A shockwave of Aetheric force erupted from his palm, colliding with the incoming spell midair. The explosion sent a concussive wave rippling across the courtyard, rattling the ground beneath their feet.

Morganna broke free of his grip, rolling to the side, and came up with her hands blazing.

She didn't hesitate.

A blast of golden light shot from her palms, slamming into the chest of the nearest Guardian. The force launched him backward, his body crumpling like paper as he collided with two more behind him.

No time to think. No time to breathe.

She spun, catching a flicker of movement—a blade arcing straight for her ribs. Instinct screamed. She threw up her arm, summoning a shield of pure light. The blade hit with bone-jarring force, sparks flying as metal met magic. The impact rattled her bones, but she held her ground.

Then Aeron was there.

He slid into place beside her, his Aether-blade crackling to life—a sleek, curved weapon forged from raw energy. He parried the next strike with ease, the clash of power ringing through the courtyard like a bell.

"You're welcome," he grunted, breathless but grinning. Morganna growled, blasting another Guardian back. "I had it." Aeron smirked, deflecting another blow. "Sure you did."

The Guardians pressed in. For every one they dropped, two more filled the space. The battle was relentless, the noise deafening—metal clashing, spells detonating, the air thick with dust and the acrid scent of burning magic.

They weren't winning.

Too many. Too fast.

Morganna's mind raced. They needed an out. Something—anything.

Her gaze snapped upward.

***

A narrow walkway stretched between two towers, suspended high above the courtyard. It was thin, precarious, and exposed—but it led straight toward the Citadel's outer parapets. Toward freedom.

"Aeron!" she shouted over the chaos. "The bridge!"

Aeron followed her gaze. Understanding flickered in his eyes instantly. No hesitation.

"Rhylen!" Aeron barked, parrying a Guardian's strike. "Can you get us up there?"

Rhylen ducked under a blade, grinning like a maniac. "Please. Watch this."

He shot his hands forward, silver-threaded magic spiraling from his fingertips like a tether. It latched onto the bridge's stone railing with a snap, anchoring the spell.

"Go!" he shouted.

Morganna didn't wait.

She sprinted, her muscles burning as she vaulted over fallen bodies and cracked stone. As she leapt, Rhylen's magic snapped tight—jerking her upward with dizzying speed.

For a heartbeat—she was flying.

The wind roared in her ears, cold and sharp against her skin.

Then—impact.

She hit the bridge hard, rolling onto her feet just as Aeron landed beside her, crouched and tense.

Rhylen followed a heartbeat later, landing far too gracefully for someone who'd just slingshot himself into the sky.

Below, the Guardians regrouped, shouting orders.

Morganna grabbed Aeron's wrist. "Move!"

They ran.

The bridge was slick with rain, the stone narrow and crumbling at the edges. The wind howled around them, threatening to throw them off with every step. But they didn't stop. They couldn't.

The parapets—freedom—were just within reach.

Then—

BOOM.

The bridge exploded.

A surge of golden energy ripped through the stone, shattering it beneath their feet. Morganna's scream was lost in the roar of the blast as the world tilted sideways.

She plummeted.

The ground rushed toward her, a yawning abyss of stone and death. She reached for the Weave—nothing. Her stomach lurched. Her lungs seized. She was falling, and this time, there was nothing to catch her.

Nothing.

Then—Aeron's hand.

He caught her mid-fall, his arm locking around her waist, the other snapping out to grab a jagged edge of the collapsing bridge. His muscles strained as he held them both, rain and sweat mixing on his face.

Morganna gasped, clinging to him.

Aeron gritted his teeth, his face twisted with effort. "I swear—you attract destruction." She laughed, breathless. "You love it." His lips twitched. "Maybe."

Then—a shadow above.

A Guardian stepped onto the fractured edge of the bridge, sword raised.

Aeron cursed. "Hold on."

And he let go.

They fell.

***

Morganna's scream was torn from her throat as they plummeted.

The world blurred around them—rain slicing past like shards of glass, the howling wind drowning out every thought. The Citadel's towering spires became streaks of shadow and light, vanishing into a storm-churned sky above.

She clung to Aeron, her fingers digging into the fabric of his tunic, feeling the frantic hammer of his heartbeat against her palm. His arm was wrapped tight around her waist, muscles straining, not with fear—he never feared—but with something fiercer. Determination.

Then—

Rhylen's magic snapped.

Silver-threaded energy whipped around them like a lasso, jerking them sideways in midair. The sudden change in momentum stole Morganna's breath, her stomach flipping as gravity twisted.

They slammed into a lower rooftop with bone-jarring force.

Morganna rolled on impact, skidding across the slick stone before slamming hard against a crumbling parapet. The breath rushed from her lungs in a painful gasp. She coughed, tasting blood in the back of her throat.

Aeron hit beside her, rolling with practiced precision, though the wince he didn't quite hide told her the fall had done more damage than he'd admit.

Rhylen landed last, of course—perfectly upright, barely ruffled. The bastard.

"Well," Rhylen panted, hands on his hips, "I'd give that landing an eight out of ten. You lost points for the screaming."

Morganna glared at him, still trying to catch her breath. "I hate you." "Admit it—you'd be dead without me." She didn't argue.

***

Aeron groaned softly, dragging himself into a sitting position. Blood trickled from a cut above his brow, mixing with the rain that had started falling harder now, washing everything in a cold, metallic scent.

Morganna crawled to him instinctively, her hands shaky as she reached for his face. Her fingers brushed the blood away, her thumb lingering against the sharp line of his jaw without thinking.

"Are you okay?" Her voice was quieter than she meant, raw and breathless.

Aeron didn't answer right away. His gray eyes locked onto hers, something fierce and vulnerable flickering in their depths—something that had nothing to do with the fall.

"I'm fine," he murmured finally, his voice rough, edged with something unsaid.

She let her hand drop, her chest tightening in a way that had nothing to do with injury.

No time for this.

She forced herself to stand, ignoring the way her knees trembled beneath her. The Citadel's spires loomed all around, jagged silhouettes against the storm-washed sky. Lights flickered in the distance—Guardians regrouping, hunting.

"They'll be here soon," Rhylen said, his tone unusually serious. "We need to move."

Morganna nodded. Her body ached, every muscle screaming, but the fire in her chest burned hotter. She wasn't done. Not even close.

She turned to Aeron, offering her hand.

He took it without hesitation, his grip strong despite the tremor she felt beneath it. When he stood, he didn't let go right away. Neither did she.

But then he did.

Because they always did.

***

They moved quickly, slipping through the Citadel's crumbling outer structures—forgotten stairwells and narrow passageways carved into the stone long before either of them had been born.

The closer they got, the more Morganna felt it.

A pull beneath her skin.

A tension in the Weave.

Like the world itself was holding its breath.

She staggered once, her hand bracing against a cold stone wall, a sudden wave of dizziness crashing over her.

Aeron was beside her instantly, his hand at her back. "Morganna—" "I'm fine," she snapped, though her heart felt like it was trying to tear itself apart.

But she wasn't fine.

The Weave was screaming.

It wasn't just fraying. It wasn't just unraveling.

It was dying.

She forced herself forward, following the invisible thread pulling her toward the truth. Toward the Heartstone.

***

They burst through the final door, the sound echoing like a thunderclap in the vast chamber beyond. The glow of the Heartstone, dimmer than she remembered.

The Heartstone floated at the center of the room, suspended above an ancient altar carved with runes that pulsed faintly with light. Golden threads of magic wove around it like veins, anchoring it to the Weave.

But Morganna's heart stopped, her feelings of the weave's pain was worsening.

When the rounded to corner, she realized it was because the Heartstone—once brilliant, radiant—was fractured.

Cracks spiderwebbed across its surface, dark veins spreading like rot. Its glow was dim, flickering like a dying star. The magic that had once been vibrant, humming with life, was now weak—thin threads unraveling into nothingness.

She staggered forward, her breath catching in her throat.

"No..."

Aeron was beside her, his face pale, his eyes wide with something she rarely saw. Fear.

Rhylen stood frozen, for once without a joke, without a grin—just silent.

Morganna's knees hit the cold stone floor.

The Weave wasn't just fraying.

The Heartstone wasn't just broken.

It was dying.

And if it died—

So did everything else.

Chapter 7

"Grief carves a wound, but rage fills it. And those who refuse to let go will learn—some threads can be rewoven, but never without a cost."

The Heartstone was dying.

Morganna stared at it, her breath trapped somewhere between disbelief and dread, her chest tightening under a pressure that had nothing to do with magic. This wasn't supposed to happen. The Heartstone was eternal—an anchor, the pulse at the core of Elysoria. It wasn't just an artifact; it was the thread from which fate itself was woven.

But now?

Fractures spiderwebbed across its surface, veins of golden light bleeding through jagged cracks. The steady hum of its power—once a constant rhythm beneath her skin—had faltered. Now it stuttered, flickering like the fading heartbeat of a dying god. Morganna felt it in her bones, in the hollow ache of her chest, in the places no magic could reach.

Aeron rose beside her, his movements slow, cautious. His storm-gray eyes—usually sharp and unshakable—were shadowed with something she'd never seen before. Not fear exactly. Something quieter. Heavier.

"Morganna," he said softly, as if her name might tether them both to reality.

She barely heard him.

Her feet moved on their own, drawn toward the fractured Heartstone like gravity itself had shifted. The air grew heavier with each step, thick with the metallic tang of magic unraveling, tasting faintly of ash and something older—like the breath of a storm just beyond the horizon. The chamber, once sacred and radiant, now felt hollow. Dead.

A low, sickly pulse rippled outward from the Heartstone. The Weave trembled in response, threads fraying at the edges of her senses. Morganna reached out, her fingers trembling as they hovered just above the fractured light.

Don't touch it, some distant voice whispered in the back of her mind.

But she did.

The moment her fingertips brushed the glowing surface, everything shattered.

A shockwave of raw, uncontrolled power exploded from the Heartstone, slamming into her with the force of a collapsing star. Morganna's body flew backward, pain lancing through every nerve as she hit the cold marble floor with a bone-jarring thud. The impact stole her breath, but it wasn't just her body that hurt. It was the world itself—cracking at the edges, the Weave screaming in protest.

She would've hit the ground harder if not for Aeron.

His arms wrapped around her mid-fall, steady despite the chaos erupting around them. His grip was firm, grounding her as her vision blurred with streaks of gold and shadow.

"Morganna!" His voice cut through the fog, raw with panic, threaded with something deeper.

She gasped, her chest heaving, but it wasn't air she was missing. It was the Weave. It wasn't just faltering—it was slipping away, the connection unraveling beneath her fingertips like sand through clenched fists.

And then the shadows moved.

At first, she thought it was just the flickering remnants of magic, the aftershocks of the Heartstone's pulse. But then they deepened—darkness folding in on itself, curling like fingers reaching from the void. The temperature plummeted, cold seeping into her bones, into her blood.

Something else was here.

Aeron's arms tightened around her before he helped her to her feet, positioning himself between her and the creeping darkness. His blade was in his hand in a flash, Aether sparking faintly along its edge—a steady, defiant glow against the encroaching shadow.

Rhylen appeared at their side, his usual grin nowhere to be found, replaced by something sharp and tense. He twirled a dagger between his fingers, though for once it wasn't for show.

"I really hate when things move that shouldn't," he muttered under his breath.

Then—

A whisper.

Low. Ancient. A voice older than language itself, woven into the very threads of reality.

"You shouldn't be here."

Morganna's heart seized. It wasn't just a voice. It was everywhere—threaded through the Weave, vibrating beneath her skin, in her blood.

The darkness rippled. Shifted.

And stepped forward.

A figure emerged from the shadows, tall and impossibly thin, its form not entirely solid—more suggestion than substance. Smoke trapped in glass. Its outline flickered, the edges frayed like reality itself couldn't hold it together. Where eyes should've been, there was nothing but endless void.

The Weave didn't bend around it.

It broke.

Aeron inhaled sharply, his stance rigid, his blade steady even as his voice dropped to a whisper.

"Kaelith."

The name felt like a curse on Morganna's tongue.

Kaelith tilted its head in an unnatural, twitching motion, as if studying them from some incomprehensible angle. Its hollow gaze locked onto Morganna. No eyes. No face. Just darkness.

"Ah... the Guardian who defies fate."

Morganna's breath caught. The Weave recoiled from him, strands snapping like brittle threads. This wasn't just an entity. It was a wound—a tear in the fabric of reality itself.

And it was here for her.

Aeron moved first.

Without hesitation, he shoved Morganna behind him, his Aether blazing brighter, his blade humming with raw power. His stance was a promise: *You'll have to go through me first.*

"Run," he said softly, his voice steady, the word a command and a plea all at once.

Morganna's jaw clenched. She could feel her magic pulsing weakly in her palms, flickering like a dying flame. But it was there.

"Like hell," she growled, stepping back beside him.

Kaelith's laugh was like the sound of glass breaking underwater—wrong in every way.

"Then let's see what fate has woven for you."

And the Devourer attacked.

***

Kaelith moved like nothing Morganna had ever faced—faster than thought, faster than fear. A blur of shadow and jagged tendrils, his form stretching and twisting as if the rules of reality were just suggestions he chose to ignore.

Morganna dove to the side just as a wave of void energy erupted from his outstretched hand. The blast tore through the chamber, leaving a jagged scar of nothingness in its wake. The Weave itself screamed, threads unraveling in the aftermath like silk shredded by claws.

Aeron was already moving, his blade singing with Aetheric energy as he lunged to intercept. The force of his strike collided with Kaelith's shadowy tendrils in an explosion of silver and black, light and darkness clashing with a sound like a thousand voices crying out at once.

The impact sent shockwaves through the chamber, cracking the marble beneath their feet.

Rhylen vanished in a flicker of shadow, reappearing behind Kaelith with a dagger aimed for what should've been a spine—if Kaelith had one. The blade pierced through the shadowy form, but instead of blood, there was only darkness, seeping around the wound like smoke.

Kaelith didn't even flinch.

A tendril lashed out, striking Rhylen with brutal force. He flew across the chamber, slamming into a pillar with a sickening crack.

"Rhylen!" Morganna shouted, but there was no time to check if he was still breathing.

Kaelith turned toward her, his formless face shifting as if amused.

"You think you matter in this story?" he whispered, his voice threading through her skull, bypassing her ears entirely. *"You are not the author. You're the ink—meant to bleed."*

Morganna's fury snapped like a whip. She raised both hands, summoning every ounce of magic she could still reach. Golden energy surged through her veins, wild and untamed. She hurled it at Kaelith in a blinding arc of light, the force of it shaking the very walls of the chamber.

It hit.

Kaelith staggered—just a fraction. But it was enough.

Aeron didn't hesitate. He was on Kaelith in an instant, blade flashing, driving it deep into the shadow's chest. The Aetheric energy flared bright and fierce, a brilliant star burning in the darkness.

Kaelith's scream wasn't a sound. It was a feeling—like grief made audible, like the echo of something ancient and dying.

But Kaelith wasn't dying.

Not yet.

With a violent surge, Kaelith retaliated, tendrils of void magic exploding outward in all directions. Aeron was thrown back, crashing into the ground with bone-jarring force.

Morganna didn't think. She ran to him, sliding to her knees, her hands already reaching for him.

"Aeron!"

He groaned, his face twisted with pain but alive. His blade was gone, knocked from his grasp, the Aetheric light dimming without its wielder's focus.

Kaelith's voice slithered through the chamber again, quieter now, but no less terrifying.

"You fight for him? For love?"

Morganna's heart thundered. She stood, placing herself between Aeron and Kaelith, her magic sparking like embers in the dark.

"Yes," she hissed, her voice trembling not with fear—but rage. "And that's what will *destroy* you."

Kaelith tilted his head, the shadows around him flickering.

"No, little Guardian."

He moved—faster than before.

Morganna raised her hands, but she was too slow.

Kaelith's shadow-blade formed mid-strike, jagged and hungry. It wasn't aimed at her.

It was aimed at Aeron.

Morganna's scream tore from her throat as she dove toward him, her magic flaring—but it was too late.

Aeron moved first.

With the last of his strength, he pushed Morganna aside, taking the full force of the blow.

The blade plunged into his chest, black veins of corruption spreading instantly from the wound.

Time fractured.

Morganna scrambled to him, her hands pressing against the wound, her magic useless against the spreading darkness. Aeron's breath hitched, his storm-gray eyes fluttering open—just enough to meet hers.

"No," she whispered, tears blurring her vision. "No, no, no—*Aeron*—"

His fingers found hers, weak but certain.

"Morganna," he rasped, blood staining his lips. "You have to—"

The Weave shuddered around them.

The Heartstone pulsed—faint and flickering, as fragile as Aeron's heartbeat beneath her hands.

And Morganna knew.

They both knew.

A sacrifice was needed.

A willing sacrifice.

Morganna shook her head, sobbing. "No. We'll find another way. We *always* find another way—"

Aeron's hand cupped her cheek, his touch feather-light but grounding. His smile was faint, filled with both sorrow and something softer—something eternal.

"I love you," he whispered. "I always have. I always will. You will find a way."

Morganna's heart broke with those words.

And then—he moved.

With the last of his strength, Aeron's hand slammed against the Heartstone.

A blinding light erupted from the impact, raw and wild, surging through the chamber like the Weave itself had been set free.

Morganna screamed, reaching for him, but the force knocked her backward.

She watched as the light wrapped around him, threads of golden energy pulling him in, unraveling him.

Unmaking him.

And then—

He was gone.

The Heartstone glowed—whole again. Restored.

The Weave hummed softly, steady once more.

But Morganna was empty.

And Kaelith's voice lingered in the silence, a final, cruel whisper etched into her soul.

"This was never about the Heartstone."

A pause. A smile in the dark.

"I was only here to watch you break."

Then he vanished, leaving nothing but echoes.

And Morganna's shattered heart.

***

The chamber was too quiet.

Morganna's breath came in ragged gasps, sharp and uneven, as if her lungs had forgotten how to work without him. She crawled forward, her trembling fingers digging into the cold marble floor where Aeron had been—*should* still be. But there was nothing. No warmth. No shadow. No trace of the man who had been her anchor, her fire, her heart.

Just... gone.

She clutched the floor as if she could pull him back through sheer force of will. Her magic sparked weakly, golden threads flickering at her fingertips, desperate and useless. It wasn't enough. It had never been enough.

The Heartstone pulsed steadily now, whole and unblemished, its glow reflecting off the tears that slid, unnoticed, down her face. It was beautiful. Perfect. Restored.

She hated it.

A sob ripped from her chest—raw, jagged, too big to contain. It echoed through the broken chamber, bouncing off the stone walls like a curse.

Rhylen appeared beside her, bruised and bloodied but alive. He dropped to his knees, his usual smirk nowhere to be found. Instead, his face was pale, hollow, like he'd lost something too. But not like *her*. Never like her.

"Morganna," he whispered, his voice rough, tentative.

She didn't respond.

What was there to say?

The Guardians gathered at the edges of the chamber, silent and stunned. Even Theron, usually composed and unreadable, looked... shaken. His sharp gaze flicked between the restored Heartstone and Morganna, but he didn't speak. He didn't have to.

This was always meant to happen.

Prophecy. Fate. Balance.

It was all just words.

None of it brought Aeron back.

Morganna's fingers curled into fists, her nails digging into her palms until she felt the sting of blood. Good. At least something still hurt.

Then she felt it—small, faint, but there.

A thread.

She glanced down.

The silver-threaded bracelet around her wrist—the one Aeron had given her years ago—glimmered softly in the dim light. It pulsed, faint and rhythmic. A heartbeat.

Her breath hitched.

He was gone. But not completely.

Her grief coiled into something sharper—something with teeth.

Not rage. Not yet.

Desperation.

Morganna didn't hesitate. Her hand shot out, fingers curling around the invisible thread of magic she felt beneath her skin, the same thread she had followed a thousand times before to call upon the Weave.

This time, it did not answer.

The air around her trembled as she reached deeper, clawing through the unseen fabric of fate, trying to pull, to grasp—to take back what had been stolen from her.

The Weave did not welcome her touch.

It recoiled.

A sharp crack split the air as her magic surged unchecked, exploding outward in a burst of raw energy. Bookshelves shattered. Ancient scrolls turned to dust in an instant. The walls trembled, the runes carved into the stone flaring with warning as the Archives themselves rejected her presence.

Pain speared through her skull, lancing down her spine like molten fire. Her body wrenched backward, flung violently across the chamber as if the very magic she had once commanded now wanted nothing to do with her.

She hit the ground hard, her breath torn from her lungs in a choked gasp. The room spun, her vision blurring at the edges.

Footsteps.

Rhylen's voice, sharp with alarm.

"Morganna!"

She barely registered his presence. Her entire body burned—not with heat, but with something worse. Something hollow.

The Weave had rejected her.

She had lost control.

And for the first time since Aeron had died, true fear crept into her bones.

Because if she couldn't wield her magic—

How the hell was she supposed to bring him back?

She stood slowly, her legs unsteady, her body screaming in protest. But she didn't care. She turned toward the Heartstone, its golden glow mocking her with its perfection.

A willing sacrifice had been needed.

And Aeron had given himself freely.

To save the world.

To save *her*.

But Morganna didn't want saving.

She wanted *him*.

She stared into the Heartstone's depths, willing it to give her something, *anything*—a sign, a flicker, a thread she could pull to unravel this cruel knot of fate. But it gave nothing back.

Nothing except silence.

Then—

A whisper.

Soft, insidious, curling around the edges of her grief like smoke seeping through a crack in the door.

"You didn't have to lose him."

Her breath caught. She spun, searching the chamber, her magic sparking weakly at her fingertips.

There, just beyond the edges of the fading shadows—Kaelith.

Not attacking. Not taunting. Just... watching.

Its form was less solid now, its edges blurring like ink bleeding into water, but its presence was unmistakable. A fracture in the world's design. A hole where something had once been.

The Guardians didn't move. Didn't even seem to see it.

Only Morganna did.

Her heart pounded in her chest, fury and grief colliding in a violent storm. She should lash out. Should burn Kaelith from existence.

But she didn't.

Because *he* was gone.

And Kaelith was still here.

A shadow carved from everything she hated—but also the only thing that hadn't left her behind.

Morganna's voice was a ragged whisper. "You did this."

Kaelith tilted its head, its hollow gaze locking onto hers. No eyes. No expression. Just endless darkness staring back.

"Did I?" The voice wasn't mocking. Not entirely. It was... curious. Almost gentle. *"I didn't force him to make that choice."*

Her throat tightened. She wanted to scream, to rip the words from the air and crush them between her fingers. But she couldn't. Because they weren't lies.

Aeron had chosen.

But Kaelith had been the architect. The quiet hand nudging pieces into place.

And now it was still here, standing in the space where Aeron should be.

"You think this was about the Heartstone?" Kaelith's voice slid through her like a blade made of ice and memory. *"No, little Guardian. This was never about the Heartstone."*

Morganna's breath hitched.

Kaelith stepped closer—not enough to threaten, just enough to be heard over the roaring silence in her chest.

"I was only here to watch you break."

The words hit harder than any blade.

But there was no magic. No threat. No battle.

Just truth.

And it worked.

Because Morganna didn't scream. Didn't fight.

She just... broke.

Something inside her snapped, silent and invisible, like a thread pulled too tight.

Kaelith didn't smile. It didn't need to.

Because it had already won.

Not through power.

Through patience.

Through grief.

Through *her*.

And as it faded into the darkness, leaving nothing but echoes behind, Morganna didn't chase it.

She just stood there, staring at the space where it had been.

Where Aeron had been.

Empty.

But not alone.

Not anymore.

***

The echoes of Kaelith's words lingered long after the shadow had vanished, woven into the very air Morganna breathed.

"I was only here to watch you break."

She stood in the hollow left behind, staring at nothing, her hands hanging useless at her sides. The weight of her grief wasn't sharp anymore. It was heavier, duller—a stone lodged beneath her ribs, pressing against every breath.

Around her, the chamber seemed to resume in slow motion. The Guardians shifted uneasily, their voices hushed whispers—anxious, unsure, as if speaking too loudly might unravel whatever fragile thread was holding Morganna together.

Rhylen approached cautiously, his usual reckless confidence nowhere to be found. He crouched beside her, his voice low and careful, like she was something fragile that might shatter if touched the wrong way.

"Morganna," he said gently.

She didn't look at him. Her gaze remained locked on the faint shimmer of dust where Kaelith had disappeared, as if staring long enough might somehow reverse time, peel back the last hour like it was just a page she could rewrite.

But this wasn't a story.

It was *real*.

And Aeron was gone.

Rhylen reached out, his hand hovering near her shoulder—but he didn't touch her. Maybe he knew better. Maybe he felt the invisible barrier she'd thrown up around herself, forged from grief and rage and something colder that she couldn't yet name.

She finally spoke, her voice hollow. "Why can I still feel him?"

Rhylen didn't answer. He couldn't.

Because she could.

Faint, distant—but there. Like an echo trapped in her bones. Like the memory of warmth after the fire's gone out.

The silver-threaded bracelet around her wrist pulsed softly, the thread of Aeron's magic woven into it like a heartbeat she couldn't quiet.

Morganna's fingers brushed over it absently.

A tether.

A thread.

Not gone.

Not yet.

She clenched her jaw, forcing herself to move. Her legs felt heavy, her muscles stiff, but she crossed the chamber until she stood beneath the Heartstone. It hovered above the altar, radiant and whole again, its golden light pulsing like nothing had ever been wrong.

But everything *was* wrong.

She hated it.

The Heartstone had demanded a sacrifice to restore balance. Aeron had given himself willingly. His life for the world. A fair trade, according to fate.

But Morganna had never believed in fair trades.

She reached for the Heartstone, her fingers brushing the air just beneath its glow. The magic hummed against her skin, familiar but distant, like a door that had been closed and locked from the other side.

It didn't feel like it had when Aeron was alive.

It didn't feel like *hers* anymore.

Her chest tightened, grief twisting into something darker.

Behind her, Theron's voice broke the silence.

"You can't bring him back."

Morganna froze, her hand hovering inches from the Heartstone. Slowly, she turned.

The High Guardian stood at the edge of the shattered floor, his expression unreadable, his piercing eyes dark with something too complicated to name. Guilt? Pity? No. Theron didn't waste time on emotions like that.

He'd known this would happen. She could see it now—in the tight set of his jaw, the rigid stance of his body.

"You knew," she whispered, her voice trembling with fury.

Theron didn't deny it. He didn't even flinch.

"I saw what needed to happen," he replied quietly. "But I couldn't interfere."

Morganna's hands curled into fists at her sides. "*Wouldn't,* you mean."

Rhylen stepped between them, tension thick in his posture. "Maybe this isn't the time—"

"*It's exactly the time,*" Morganna snapped, her voice sharp enough to cut.

She stormed toward Theron, stopping only when they were a breath apart. Her magic pulsed faintly, golden light flickering beneath her skin like embers waiting for fuel.

"You let him die," she hissed. "You watched it happen."

Theron's gaze didn't waver. "It was the only way."

The words felt like a slap.

Morganna staggered back, shaking her head. She couldn't listen to this. Not now. Maybe not ever.

She turned away, her heart pounding like war drums against her ribs.

But the words Kaelith had left her with wouldn't fade.

"I was only here to watch you break."

And she *was* breaking.

But not in the way Kaelith had expected.

Not shattered.

Not destroyed.

Changed.

Her grief was a blade now, honed and sharp.

And she knew what she had to do.

She faced Theron again, her voice steady despite the storm raging inside her.

"There's a way to bring him back."

Rhylen's head snapped toward her, his eyes wide. "Morganna—"

"There's always a way," she continued, cutting him off. "Magic this old doesn't disappear. It transforms. It shifts." She pointed to the Heartstone, her expression cold. "It took him. It can give him back."

Theron's face darkened. "You're talking about *unraveling* fate itself."

Morganna's smile was sharp and bitter. "Then I guess I'll need to learn how."

She turned, not waiting for their protests.

She didn't care.

They'd let Aeron go.

But she wouldn't.

Not now.

Not ever.

And somewhere, in the lingering shadows at the edges of the chamber, something *watched*.

And it smiled.

Chapter 8

"The storm is not in the sky. It is in the choices we make, the paths we refuse to walk, and the truths we cannot bear to face."

The Heartstone was whole again. The Weave was restored. The world had been saved.

And Morganna had never felt more hollow.

She stood in the ruins left after the battle, surrounded by golden light and hollow voices—faint echoes of triumph that rang false in her ears. The restored Heartstone pulsed steadily above the altar, flawless and unmarred, as if none of it had ever happened. As if *he* had never been there at all.

"Aeron."

His name was a ghost now, one she didn't dare speak aloud.

The Guardians gathered in quiet clusters around the edges of the chamber, their whispers low but persistent.

"They did it." "They saved us all." "The Heartstone lives because of her."

A savior.

The word echoed like poison in Morganna's mind.

She clenched her fists, her nails biting into her palms as if pain might anchor her to something real. How *dare* they speak of salvation? How dare the world continue spinning, the Weave humming softly beneath her feet, when Aeron's heartbeat had been stolen from her?

How dare the Heartstone stand whole while she was shattered?

A hand settled gently on her shoulder. She didn't flinch. She didn't even blink.

Theron's voice was a controlled murmur, careful and calculated. "Morganna, you should rest."

Rest.

The word tasted like ash.

He said it like she was tired. Like exhaustion was the thing hollowing her out instead of grief sharpened into a blade. Like she was still the girl she'd been before—before her heart had been carved out of her chest and offered up to fate like some meaningless sacrifice.

Slowly, she turned.

The Guardians were watching her with reverence, their expressions painted with awe and fragile gratitude. They didn't see her. Not really. To them, she was a symbol—a living monument to victory.

None of them had fought for him. None of them had tried to stop this. None of them had bled the way she had.

Her throat tightened, raw and jagged.

"I don't need rest," Morganna whispered, her voice brittle as shattered glass.

Theron's gaze flickered, something like concern—or maybe guilt—etched into the faint lines around his eyes. "Morganna—"

Her magic surged before he could finish, golden tendrils sparking at her fingertips. The torches lining the walls flickered violently, casting distorted shadows that clawed up the stone like fingers reaching for something just out of grasp. The Heartstone's glow dimmed for a heartbeat, shrinking beneath the weight of her fury.

Theron froze. His words faltered.

Good.

"You know nothing," she murmured, her voice soft but searing, like embers buried under ash.

For the first time, Theron looked afraid.

Good.

She turned away. She had nothing left to say.

***

The next three days passed like a fever dream.

Morganna didn't remember the ceremonies. Didn't acknowledge the celebrations. Didn't speak. Didn't eat. Didn't sleep.

She was the *hero* of the Citadel. The Guardian who saved the world. The one who restored balance.

And none of it mattered.

The whispers began on the fourth night.

She sat alone on the narrow balcony outside her chambers, the distant stars sharp against the black velvet sky. The city below buzzed softly with life, oblivious to the emptiness sitting in her chest like a stone. Her fingers twisted the silver-threaded bracelet wrapped around her wrist—the one Aeron had given her. The only piece of him she had left.

The wind shifted. Cold. Sharp.

And then—

"You could undo this."

Morganna froze.

The voice wasn't real. It couldn't be.

But it slid through her mind like silk, soft and poisonous, curling around her thoughts with the familiarity of something that had always been there—just waiting.

"The Weave does not end with loss." "The Heartstone bends to those who dare reshape it." "You could bring him back."

She exhaled slowly, her grip tightening around the bracelet until the threads bit into her skin. "No."

The wind laughed. A sound that wasn't wind at all.

"No? Or... not yet?"

Her eyes burned, stinging with something she refused to name. She squeezed them shut, pressing the bracelet to her chest like it could keep the darkness out.

But the whisper had already done its damage.

Because now— Now, the thought existed.

The question was real. And no matter how much she tried to ignore it— She couldn't unhear it.

She curled into herself, her heart a hollow, aching thing.

Aeron's last words echoed in her mind, soft and steady.

"This isn't the end."

She buried her face in her hands.

And for the first time since he had died— Morganna wept.

***

Morganna stood at the edge of the Sanctum of Balance, her silhouette carved against the golden glow of the restored Heartstone. The vast chamber echoed with faint whispers of the Weave's power, woven seamlessly through the stone beneath her feet. Reflections of light rippled in the still pools below, fractured by tremors that only she seemed to feel.

Her hands gripped the cold stone railing, her knuckles bone-white. The strain in her fingers grounded her, anchoring her to *something*—anything—while the rest of her unraveled quietly beneath the surface.

The Savior of Elysoria. The Guardian who defied the darkness. The woman who saved the Heartstone.

That's what they called her. That's who they thought she was.

But they didn't know. They didn't know the truth.

Aeron's sacrifice wasn't noble. It wasn't a grand, fated choice. It was a theft. It had been ripped from him. From her.

Her breath hitched. She squeezed her eyes shut, furious with herself. She hadn't cried since that night—not again. Not after she'd buried her heart alongside his in the remnants of the Heartstone's shattered glow.

And then—

"You could undo this."

The whisper slid through her mind like a blade, soft and sharp all at once.

Morganna's grip on the railing tightened, her nails carving faint grooves into the stone. "Leave me alone," she hissed under her breath.

Silence. For a heartbeat.

Then—laughter.

Not loud. Not mocking. Soft. Like an old friend.

"Is that what you want?"

Her fingers trembled. Because she didn't know.

She didn't know what she wanted anymore.

She had saved the world. She had won.

Then why did it feel like she'd lost everything that mattered?

***

She didn't hear him enter. She simply felt it—a ripple in the Weave, faint and familiar, like the subtle shift in air pressure before a storm.

Morganna didn't turn. Her eyes remained fixed on the flickering reflection of the Heartstone in the pools below, its golden light fractured and distorted, just like everything else.

"You shouldn't be here alone," came Theron's voice, smooth and precise, each word placed with care—as if that could contain the damage already done.

She exhaled slowly, her breath a thin stream of frost in the cold chamber. "You sound concerned."

His footsteps echoed softly as he crossed the stone floor, deliberate and measured. His reflection appeared beside hers in the water, tall and imposing, robes dark against the Heartstone's glow.

"I am."

Morganna's laugh was a brittle thing, sharp enough to cut. "Now? After everything?"

Theron's silence was louder than any answer.

She finally turned to face him, her gaze a blade honed by grief. The man before her was a ghost of the mentor she'd once trusted. His face was as composed as ever, carved from stone, but she could see it—the faint lines around his eyes, the tension stitched into his posture.

Guilt.

"You knew," she whispered. Not a question. A fact.

Theron didn't deny it. His eyes met hers, unflinching. "I did."

The admission punched the air from her lungs. Not because it was surprising—but because it wasn't.

"And you let it happen."

His jaw tightened, a flicker of something—regret?—flashing behind his carefully controlled expression. "I couldn't interfere."

Couldn't or *wouldn't*?

Morganna's magic flared at her fingertips, thin threads of golden light dancing across her skin like cracks in fragile porcelain. She wanted to scream, to tear down the walls, to *unmake* the world that had cost her everything.

But she didn't.

Instead, she smiled. A slow, sharp curve of her lips—cold and hollow.

"Because of the prophecy," she said softly, tasting the bitterness in every syllable.

Theron nodded once. "It was foretold long before you were born. A Guardian's love would lead to the unraveling of the Weave."

Her breath hitched. The words landed like a blade between her ribs.

A Guardian's love.

Aeron.

Morganna's voice dropped to a whisper. "You thought it would be him."

Theron's silence was all the confirmation she needed.

Her hands clenched into fists. "And now you think it's me."

Theron stepped closer, his gaze sharp and unyielding. "I don't think. I *know*."

She didn't move. Didn't flinch.

"If you refuse to let go," he continued quietly, "you will be the one who breaks the world."

Morganna stared at him for a long moment, the echoes of his words stitching themselves into the cracks of her heart.

Then she tilted her head slightly, her smile widening just enough to show teeth.

"Then you'd better pray," she whispered, her voice soft as silk and sharp as glass, "that I never decide to stop saving it."

She turned her back on him—and walked away.

***

The Chamber of Threads was quieter than it had ever been. Gone was the hum—the soft, melodic thrum of magic that used to pulse beneath Morganna's skin like a second heartbeat. Now, it was hollow. A cathedral stripped of its gods, sacred only in the way grief can make anything feel sacred.

She stood alone at the center of the room, surrounded by cascading strands of golden light—threads of fate, suspended like fragile ribbons in the dim glow of flickering torches. They should've responded to her presence, should've leaned into her touch like they always had. The Weave had been her constant, her anchor, her gift. Now, it was a stranger. Silent. Cold.

Her fingers hovered inches from the nearest thread, trembling with something she refused to name. Fear. Not of the Weave. Not of failure. Of the answer she might find—or worse, the one she wouldn't.

She took a breath. Steeled herself. And reached out.

At first, nothing happened.

The thread was cool beneath her fingertips, slick like water slipping through cracks she couldn't seal. She tried to grasp it, to pull it the way she had countless times before, but it resisted. Slippery. Unyielding. Her magic flickered—faint, brittle—a shadow of what it had once been.

"*Come on,*" Morganna whispered, her jaw clenched, fingers curling tighter around the fragile strand. She poured more magic into it, trying to coax the thread to respond, to feel something—anything.

A flicker. A spark. And then—

A voice.

"*Morganna...*"

She froze. Her heart stuttered. That voice—faint, distant, like a whisper carried on a dying wind. But she knew it. She would know it anywhere. *Aeron.*

Her knees nearly buckled, a choked breath escaping her lips. She yanked at the thread, desperate to hear it again, to pull it closer, to drag it back from wherever it was hiding. Her magic surged recklessly, wild and sharp, unraveling threads she wasn't strong enough to control.

"*Aeron!*" she screamed, her voice ragged, raw with need.

The Weave bucked. Violent. Unforgiving.

Magic snapped like taut strings tearing under too much pressure. A blast of raw energy exploded from the tangled threads, slamming into her chest and hurling her backward. She hit the stone floor with a sickening crack, her breath knocked from her lungs.

Silence fell. But not the peaceful kind. The empty kind.

Morganna lay there, gasping, the metallic tang of blood flooding her mouth. She wiped at her face, her trembling fingers coming away streaked with red. Blood dripped from her nose, trailing down her chin, staining the pristine floor of the chamber.

She stared at it. At the fragile, fragile thing she'd become.

"The Weave won't give him back."

The voice wasn't Aeron's this time. It was smoother. Colder. A velvet blade slipping between her ribs.

Kaelith.

She didn't look for him. Didn't need to. His presence coiled around her like smoke, invisible but suffocating. She could feel him in the shadows, lurking at the edges of her ruin.

"*But I can,*" he murmured, soft as sin.

Morganna's breath hitched, her fingers tightening around nothing. Her blood still dripped, warm against her skin, but she didn't care. She was too empty to feel the sting.

She forced herself to sit up, her body trembling with exhaustion, with fury. She looked down at her blood-streaked hands—once capable of weaving fate itself—and felt something sharp and poisonous bloom in her chest.

Not grief. Not sorrow. Rage.

She rose to her feet, swaying slightly, her eyes burning—not with tears, but with the embers of something darker.

She turned toward the shadows, toward Kaelith's voice, her face a mask carved from glass and fury.

"Then I don't need the Weave."

The words tasted like ash and power on her tongue. And for the first time since Aeron's death, she felt something that wasn't hollow. She felt free.

***

Morganna didn't return to her chambers.

She wandered the dark corridors of the Citadel, her footsteps echoing like distant thunder. The halls were empty at this hour, the flickering torches casting long, distorted shadows that danced along the stone walls.

Her mind spun, tangled with grief and rage, guilt and longing. She felt like she was unraveling—thread by thread—until there was nothing left but the hollow ache where Aeron's presence used to be.

"You know the truth now, don't you?"

The whisper slid through her thoughts like oil, smooth and suffocating.

Morganna's jaw clenched. She didn't respond. Didn't need to. The voice wasn't waiting for permission.

"They let him die." "They feared your love more than they feared the unraveling itself."

She stopped walking.

The corridor was dark, lit only by the faint golden glow of distant torches. She stood there, trembling—not from fear, but from the weight of everything she couldn't carry anymore.

"But you could change that."

Her hands curled into fists. She wanted to scream, to tear the words from the air, to *erase* the thought before it could take root.

But it was too late.

Because it was already there. A seed planted in the soil of her grief.

And it was growing.

Morganna's steps turned, almost without her realizing it, leading her deeper into the Citadel's heart—toward the forbidden archives.

The torches dimmed as she passed, shadows thickening like they *recognized* her. Like they welcomed her.

The ancient door loomed ahead, carved with runes meant to keep secrets buried. Wards designed to lock away forbidden knowledge.

Knowledge about the Weave. About the Heartstone. About *undoing* what had been done.

She reached for the door.

No hesitation. No fear.

The shadows seemed to sigh as it creaked open.
And Morganna stepped inside.

Chapter 9

"Some wounds do not fester. They do not scream. They do not warn you of their rot. Some wounds simply exist—until one day, you realize they have already consumed you."

The Heartstone pulsed softly now—steady and whole, as if nothing had happened. But something had. Something irreversible.

Aeron was gone.

The echoes of battle had long faded. The Citadel's fractured walls had been rebuilt, the scars on its stone scrubbed clean. The Weave had been patched, its golden threads humming with fragile precision, like nothing had ever frayed. The Guardians—those who survived—returned to their duties, their oaths stitched back into neat, familiar routines.

But for Rhylen, time hadn't moved at all.

It was still that moment. That final breath. That last, impossible choice.

"I love you. I always have. I always will. You'll find a way."

The words haunted him more than the silence that followed. Because Aeron wasn't supposed to be gone. Not him. Not the boy who never lost a fight. Not the reckless Guardian who defied rules like breathing. Not his best friend. His brother in all but blood.

And now, the space Aeron left behind was a chasm—one Rhylen had no idea how to fill.

***

Rhylen stood at the edge of the training grounds, the same dusty stretch where he and Aeron had sparred a thousand times. The ground was etched with faint footprints that would fade soon enough—just like everything else.

Morganna wasn't there. She hadn't been back since the day Aeron died.

She moved through the Citadel like a shadow stitched to someone else's life—silent, untethered, not really *there* at all. Her golden magic, once fierce and unruly, had dimmed to a faint, brittle glow. Her voice had become a rumor.

And it was killing him to watch.

Rhylen could handle loss. He'd faced it before—friends, battles, moments stolen by fate's careless hand. But this? Watching *her* disappear? No. He'd lost Aeron. He wasn't going to lose Morganna too.

***

Morganna stood at the ruined balcony of the Watchtower, staring into the abyss where the sky should have been.

Wind howled through the cracks in the stone, pulling at the edges of her cloak, whispering secrets in the language of ghosts. The battlefield stretched far below—a graveyard of fallen banners and broken weapons, remnants of a war she had not been there to stop.

She felt Rhylen before she heard him.

He didn't speak at first.

Didn't need to.

His presence alone was a challenge—a silent reminder of the path she had left behind.

"Say it," Morganna muttered, arms crossed tightly over her chest. Her voice was sharper than she intended.

Rhylen stepped closer, his boots scraping against the worn stone. "Say what?"

"That I should stop. That I should turn back. That I'm making a mistake."

He exhaled through his nose. "Would it matter if I did?"

Silence.

Morganna clenched her fists, nails biting into her palms.

"That's what I thought," she said flatly, her throat tight.

Rhylen watched her carefully, studying every flicker of expression that crossed her face. "I don't need to tell you that you're making a mistake, Morganna. You already know."

She whirled on him, violet fire crackling in her eyes. "I don't know anything anymore, Rhylen! Don't you get that? Aeron is gone. The Weave took him, and we—" Her voice broke before she could stop it.

Rhylen flinched. Not at her anger. At her pain.

Morganna sucked in a sharp breath, shoving it down, hard.

She straightened, every inch of her locking into place like armor. "I don't need saving."

Rhylen's jaw ticked.

"No," he agreed quietly. "You need to stop running before there's nothing left of you to save."

The words struck deeper than any blade.

Morganna swallowed hard, forcing herself to look away.

She had no answer for him. No defense.

So she left.

And Rhylen let her go.

***

The training grounds had always been filled with sound.

The ring of steel. The clash of magic. The echo of laughter.

But not tonight.

Tonight, the space was empty.

Rhylen stood alone on the worn training mats, running his hand over the familiar grooves in the stone—the same ones that had been there for years, carved by endless sparring sessions.

His fingers brushed against a deep gouge near the center, a scar in the floor from Aeron's sword slamming into the ground after Morganna had knocked him flat on his ass.

Rhylen could still hear it—the laughter.

Could still see it.

***

"You're too damn fast," Aeron grumbled, rolling onto his back, staring at the sky. His sword lay useless beside him.

"No," Morganna smirked, planting the tip of her blade into the dirt, grinning down at him. "You're just slow."

"I'll show you slow, Guardian of Smugness," Aeron muttered, reaching for his sword.

But Rhylen beat him to it.

"Nope," he said, snatching the weapon and twirling it lazily. *"Winner keeps the blade. House rules."*

Aeron groaned dramatically. "I swear, you two just make up rules as you go."

"Obviously," Morganna said, her smirk widening. "That's why we always win."_

Aeron looked between them, narrowed his eyes. Then—

He lunged for Rhylen, tackling him to the ground in a mess of limbs and laughter, swearing something about cheating bastards and eternal grudges.

Morganna had stood above them, arms crossed, shaking her head.

"Children," she sighed. *"I train with children."*

"You love us," Aeron had shot back, grinning up at her.

Rhylen had laughed—had truly laughed, warm and reckless, the sound easy in a way he hadn't known could be temporary.

And Morganna—

She had just rolled her eyes.

But her smile had given her away.

***

The echo of laughter faded as Rhylen stood alone on the training grounds, the space around him too quiet, too still.

The stone beneath his boots was cold.

The training mats were empty.

And Aeron was gone.

But Morganna wasn't.

Not yet.

His hands clenched at his sides.

Not yet.

Then—the war horns sounded.

The first battle of the Shadow War had begun.

***

Morganna stood at the battlefield's edge, shadow coiling around her like a storm barely contained.

The enemy forces moved in waves, creatures of darkness twisted by the corruption bleeding through the remnants of the Heartstone. Elysoria's Guardians stood opposite them, weapons drawn, their magic pulsing with desperate resolve.

But Morganna—

She was not with them.

She was alone.

A force unto herself.

The battle roared to life, steel meeting steel, magic tearing through the night. Morganna raised her hands, dark power flaring to life, and for the first time, she stopped hesitating.

The moment she stepped forward—the moment she struck—

There was no turning back.

Chapter 10

"The dead are never truly gone. They linger in the spaces between heartbeats, in the echoes of words left unsaid, waiting for someone to listen."

The Weave had been restored. The world was whole again.

And yet—Morganna felt like a ghost living in it.

She stood before the Heartstone, its golden glow pulsing in steady, rhythmic waves, like the heartbeat of a world that didn't care what it had taken to survive. The fractures that once marred its surface were gone, smoothed over by the price Aeron had paid. It pulsed with balance. With stability.

It should have felt right. But all she wanted was to tear it apart again.

Her fingers curled into fists, nails digging crescent moons into her palms. The steady hum beneath her skin was quieter now—like the Weave itself knew what had been lost but refused to acknowledge it.

She had returned to the Citadel's routines—the rigid structure of Guardian duties, the endless hours of training, the sterile lectures on fate, balance, and duty. She slipped back into it with mechanical precision, her steps practiced, her words clipped, her magic sharp as ever.

But none of it mattered. Not anymore.

She had saved the world. And yet, without him, it meant nothing.

***

The first time Morganna attempted to weave a new fate after the battle, her hands shook.

She knelt in the Chamber of Threads, the air thick with the soft hum of golden strands suspended in the dim light. They floated around her like fragile ribbons of destiny, each one humming with life, with possibility.

This was supposed to be familiar. But it wasn't.

She reached out, her fingers ghosting over the threads. For as long as she could remember, the Weave had been a constant hum beneath her skin—a song only she could hear. It had been her anchor, her purpose.

But now— Now, it was quiet.

Not dead. Not broken. Just... hollow.

She swallowed hard, her throat dry, and forced herself to touch the strands. They responded—but sluggishly, hesitant, as if unsure whether to trust her. Like they knew. Like they remembered. Like the Weave itself had felt Aeron's absence, too.

Her breath hitched.

"You'll find a way for us, Morganna."

His voice. His voice.

She recoiled as if burned, jerking back so violently that the threads snapped loose from her grasp, unraveling into sparks of light that faded into the air.

Her heart thundered. She wasn't breathing—Gods, she wasn't breathing.

The chamber blurred, golden strands dimming around her as her vision swam with unshed tears. She heard distant voices, the concerned murmurs of other Guardians turning to look at her.

Morganna staggered to her feet, her legs unsteady. "I need air." She fled before anyone could stop her.

***

She found herself on a balcony overlooking the endless sprawl of Elysoria, the city below glittering like a field of stars. The cold wind bit at her skin, sharp and unforgiving, but she welcomed the sting.

She wasn't alone.

"You heard him."

Morganna froze. The whisper coiled around her like smoke, invisible but suffocating. She gritted her teeth, forcing herself to stare straight ahead, refusing to give it power.

"You heard his voice in the Weave."

She squeezed her eyes shut, her nails digging deeper into her palms until they drew blood.

"Because he is still there."

A tremor rippled through her chest.

The worst part wasn't that the whisper lied. The worst part was that it sounded so terribly, perfectly right.

***

If Morganna was drowning, Rhylen was the only one who noticed.

He didn't talk about Aeron. Didn't speak his name, didn't reference the shadow that hung between them. But he stayed. He trained beside her. He walked with her through the Citadel halls. He matched her pace, adjusted his stride, filled the silences she never wanted to acknowledge.

But it wasn't the same. It would never be the same.

And that was worse than if he had done nothing at all.

One evening, as they stood overlooking the Citadel walls, Rhylen finally broke the silence. "You know," he said quietly, his voice rough from disuse, "you're allowed to be angry."

Morganna exhaled sharply through her nose. "I'm not angry."

Rhylen tilted his head slightly, his sharp gaze pinning her. "Then what are you?"

She hated him for asking. Hated that he saw through her, saw the cracks she'd tried so hard to seal shut.

But she had no answer.

Because what was she, now that Aeron was gone?

She turned away, her jaw clenched. Rhylen didn't stop her. He never did.

***

Weeks passed.

Morganna spent more time in the training grounds, sometimes alone, sometimes with Rhylen. Her blade became an extension of herself, her magic a reflex she didn't think about anymore.

One night, unable to sleep, she found herself back in the chamber where Aeron had once trained. The faint scorch marks on the walls, remnants of old battles, were still there—ghosts etched into stone.

She ran her fingers over one of the marks, her heart tightening.

"You always overreach on the second strike," Aeron had teased her once, laughing as he'd dodged effortlessly.

She closed her eyes, letting the memory cut deeper than any blade could.

Without thinking, she summoned a pulse of magic, slashing it across the wall in a burst of golden fire. The stone cracked, dust spilling to the floor.

It wasn't enough.

She kept going—strike after strike, her magic burning hot, wild, reckless. Until her arms trembled and her breath came in ragged gasps. Until her knees gave out.

Until she was nothing but ash inside.

***

Rhylen found her the next morning, slumped against the scorched wall, her hands bloody from gripping her blade too tightly.

He didn't say anything at first. Just stood there, taking in the wreckage she'd left behind.

Then—softly— "You're getting worse."

Morganna let out a bitter breath, the faintest ghost of a laugh. "You always were observant."

Rhylen didn't smile. Didn't laugh. "You heard him, didn't you?"

Her breath caught. She didn't respond. Didn't need to.

Rhylen exhaled sharply, raking a hand through his hair. "Morganna—"

She cut him off. "Don't."

He didn't listen. "Theron was right," he said quietly. "You have to let him go."

The words hit her like a blade. Let him go. Let Aeron go.

Like he was something that could be released. Like he was something that could be forgotten.

She turned her head slowly, her eyes sharp and burning.

"If you want to take his place so badly, Rhylen, just say it."

His face didn't change. But something in his eyes did. A flicker of pain. A flicker of understanding.

He sighed softly. "That's not what this is."

Morganna turned away. "Then stop acting like it is."

Rhylen didn't argue. He just stayed. Sat there beside her, in the silence, where nothing could be fixed.

***

That night, Morganna returned to the Chamber of Threads.

She told herself it was to clear her mind. To feel something familiar. To breathe.

Instead, she sat alone beneath the flickering golden strands of fate, her fingers ghosting over them, her heart hollow.

The Weave had always been a song beneath her skin. A living thing that answered her call. But now, it was silent. No—not silent. Incomplete.

Like a thread had been pulled loose. Like something was missing.

Her hands trembled as she reached out.

And for the second time, she heard it.

"Morganna."

She gasped, her fingers snapping back as if burned. Her heart slammed against her ribs, her breath ragged and shallow.

That voice. She knew that voice.

She'd heard it in stolen moments, in soft laughter under moonlight, in whispered promises she thought would last forever.

Aeron.

The Weave shivered beneath her fingertips. Golden light flickered at the edges of her vision.

"Morganna."

She stumbled to her feet, fleeing the chamber before the whispers could follow.

***

"You heard him."

Morganna stood in the darkness of her chambers, staring out at the city below. She didn't answer. She didn't have to.

The whisper coiled around her like a lover's touch, soft and familiar.

"Because he is still there."

Her breath hitched.

"You could bring him back."

She shut her eyes tightly, shaking her head. "No."

The whisper sighed, almost tender.

"Not yet, then."

And that was the worst part. It didn't press. It didn't demand. It just waited.

***

Kaelith had all the time in the world.

It had taken centuries for the Weave to strengthen him again. It had taken years for the Guardians to forget what had once nearly destroyed them.

And now— It had only to wait. Wait for Morganna to break. Wait for her to fall. Wait for her to finally say yes.

Because she would. And when she did— She would be his.

Chapter 11

"Some doors, once opened, cannot be closed. The question is not whether you should step through—it's whether you'll recognize yourself on the other side."

Morganna was tired of pretending. Tired of acting like she was whole, like she could still be the Guardian they wanted her to be. She had tried. Gods, she had tried.

Tried to return to the Weave. Tried to train. Tried to be Morganna the Luminous.

But every time she reached for the magic—she heard him. *"Morganna."* Every time she looked at Rhylen—she felt guilt. Every time she closed her eyes—the whispers were waiting.

And she was so damn tired.

***

Three nights passed without sleep. It was easier that way.

No dreams. No memories. No whispers she wasn't ready to hear.

She roamed the Citadel like a shadow slipping between walls of stone, her footsteps silent on marble floors carved with ancient runes. The torches burned low, casting long fingers of light that reached for her but never touched.

Her path wasn't random. It never was. Even when she told herself it was.

Tonight, her steps led her back to the Chamber of Threads.

The door creaked softly as it closed behind her, swallowing the faint sounds of the Citadel. She stood alone, surrounded by the Weave—golden strands suspended in the dim light, humming softly, like threads stitched into the fabric of the universe. They should've felt like home.

But they felt like strangers.

Morganna stepped forward, her hands trembling as she reached for them. The threads shifted, reacting to her touch—not with warmth, but with hesitation. Like the Weave itself had learned to fear her.

She swallowed the knot in her throat and forced her fingers to close around a strand.

"Morganna."

She flinched.

The thread slipped from her grasp, snapping back with a faint, metallic hum. Around her, the strands flickered, responding to the sharp spike of emotion she couldn't suppress.

But this wasn't just grief. The whisper was clearer this time. Closer.

Aeron.

Her breath hitched. She squeezed her eyes shut, her chest tight. "Aeron?" she whispered, her voice shaking.

The Weave shuddered.

For a heartbeat—he was there. A flicker of golden light. A thread stretched too thin. And gods—*she felt him.*

His warmth. His presence. His heartbeat tangled with hers.
Then— Gone.

The absence hit like a blade, sharp and cruel. She gasped, stumbling back, her hands clutching at empty air.

No. No, she'd felt him. He was still here. Trapped. Calling to her. *Waiting.*

Her pulse roared in her ears. Her fingers curled into fists.

She wasn't losing her mind. She was wasting time.

***

At dawn, she packed what little she needed—her blades, a map etched with forgotten paths, and a heart already fractured beyond repair.

She didn't expect to be stopped. She should've known better.

Rhylen caught her just past the Citadel gates.

"Morganna."

His voice was soft. Tired. Like he'd been waiting.

She didn't turn around. Didn't want to see the look on his face—the one filled with things she couldn't bear to feel.

"Don't," she said flatly.

He ignored her, stepping closer. "You don't have to do this alone."

Her jaw clenched. *Alone?* She wasn't alone. She had Aeron. She could hear him. She just had to find him.

She took another step forward. His hand shot out, gripping her arm.

"Morganna," he rasped, his voice sharper now. "*Look at me.*"

She froze.

Slowly—too slowly—she turned to face him.

Rhylen's eyes weren't filled with anger or frustration. They were filled with something worse. *Fear.*

"You think I don't know what you're doing?" he whispered. "I see it every time you walk away. You're not looking for answers. You're looking for a way to undo what happened."

Her throat tightened.

"I'm not—" she started. *Liar.*

"You are." His grip tightened just enough to make her feel it. "And it's going to kill you."

She ripped her arm free. "Then let it."

The words hung in the air, sharp and final.

Rhylen didn't move. Didn't argue.

But his voice was soft when he finally spoke. "I already lost him, Morganna. I won't lose you too."

She swallowed hard, her chest aching. But she couldn't afford to feel it. Not now. So she turned. And kept walking.

Rhylen didn't follow. But she felt his gaze long after he was gone.

***

The ruins of the Veiled Sanctum were carved into the jagged cliffs beyond the Reach, hidden beneath layers of earth and enchantments designed to be forgotten.

But Morganna had never forgotten.

This was where the first Guardians buried their secrets—knowledge too dangerous to destroy, too powerful to trust in the wrong hands.

She crossed the threshold without hesitation, her footsteps echoing in hollow chambers where echoes didn't belong.

The walls were etched with faded runes, their meanings lost to time. Dust coated the air, thick and heavy, clinging to her skin like ash.

She descended deeper, guided by nothing but instinct. Or maybe something else.

At the heart of the Sanctum, she found it.

A book. Untouched by time. Bound in dark leather, stitched with threads that shimmered like shadows.

Her hands trembled as she reached for it. She shouldn't. She knew that.

But she did.

The moment her fingers touched the cover—

"Ah, little Guardian."

The voice slithered through the darkness, soft and venomous.

"Finally."

Morganna's breath caught. She spun around— But there was no one there.

Just the shadows. And the whisper that was not Aeron.

"I've been waiting."

And the worst part?

So had she.

***

Morganna's pulse thundered in her ears, her hand still resting on the dark, ancient tome. The cover was cold beneath her fingertips—not the chill of stone, but something deeper. A cold that sank past skin and bone, something *hungry*.

She forced herself to breathe. Steady. Control.

"Who's there?" she demanded, her voice sharper than she felt.

Silence answered. Then—

"You know me."

The whisper slid through the ruins like smoke, threading through the cracks in the stone, seeping into her thoughts. It wasn't loud. It didn't need to be.

She did know. *Kaelith.*

She didn't speak his name. Speaking it felt like giving him power. Instead, she stepped back from the pedestal where the book rested, her hand falling to the hilt of her blade.

A laugh answered her—soft, amused, like the rustle of dead leaves.

"Still clinging to the sword, little Guardian?" the voice purred. *"As if steel could protect you from what's already inside."*

The shadows thickened around her, stretching unnaturally, pressing in like a tide.

Morganna swallowed hard, her jaw clenched. "You're wasting your time."

"Am I?"

The air grew colder, heavy with the scent of ash and something faintly metallic—like blood long dried.

"You've heard him," Kaelith whispered. *"Felt him. Even now, his voice echoes in your mind."*

Morganna's fingers tightened around the hilt of her blade. "You're lying."

"No." The word was a soft hiss. *"I don't need to lie. You've already done the hardest part for me."*

She shook her head, stepping back toward the exit, toward the faint sliver of light beyond the cracked archway.

But the shadows followed.

"You came here for answers, Morganna." His voice coiled around her like a serpent, low and intimate. *"And you found them."*

She spun, slashing her blade through the darkness— But it passed through nothing. Just cold air and silence.

And then—

"Do you know why you can still hear him?"

She froze. Her heart stuttered in her chest.

"Because he's not gone."

The blade slipped from her fingers, clattering against the stone floor with a hollow, metallic ring.

Not gone.

Morganna's breath hitched, her knees nearly buckling.

"He's trapped," Kaelith whispered, his voice softer now, almost gentle. *"Caught between the Weave and the Heartstone. Suspended. Waiting."*

Her vision blurred, tears stinging the corners of her eyes.

"You feel it, don't you? That ache beneath your ribs? That pull when you reach for the Weave?" A pause, a breath. *"That's him."*

Her hand drifted unconsciously to her chest, where the pain lived like a second heartbeat.

"I can help you," Kaelith murmured. *"I can show you how to bring him back."*

Morganna squeezed her eyes shut, shaking her head. "You're lying."

"Am I?"

Silence stretched between them, thick and suffocating.

Then—

"You've felt it. You've heard him. And yet... you do nothing. You let him remain there, lost, suffering, because you're too afraid to face what it will cost to save him."

Morganna crumpled to her knees, her fingers digging into the cold stone floor.

She wanted to scream. She wanted to tear the words from her mind. But she couldn't. Because they were already there.

Kaelith didn't press. Didn't rush. He just... waited.

***

Morganna stayed there for what felt like hours, the shadows pressing in, the weight of his words sinking deeper.

Eventually, her fingers brushed the edge of the book again. She stared at it. At the dark, pulsing ink stitched into its cover like veins.

Her hands trembled as she picked it up. It was heavier than she expected, the weight of it anchoring her, grounding her.

She didn't open it. Not yet.

But she didn't put it down, either.

"When you're ready," Kaelith whispered, his voice fading like a dying ember, *"I'll be here."*

And he was. Even after the shadows receded, even after the echoes of his voice faded— He was still there. Waiting.

***

When Morganna returned to the Citadel, dawn was breaking—pale light spilling over the horizon, too soft, too indifferent to the storm inside her.

She slipped through the gates unnoticed, her cloak drawn tight around her shoulders, the forbidden book hidden beneath its folds.

She found Rhylen in the training grounds, already awake, his blade flashing in the morning light. He froze when he saw her.

"Morganna," he said quietly, his eyes narrowing. "Where have you been?"

She didn't answer. Couldn't.

He crossed the distance between them in three long strides, his hand catching her arm. His fingers tightened when he felt her trembling.

His gaze dropped to the faint, dark marks on her skin—like threads of shadow etched beneath the surface.

Too late, she thought distantly.

Rhylen's voice was sharp now, filled with something dangerously close to fear. "What did you do?"

She pulled her arm free, her expression cold and empty. "Nothing you can fix."

She turned to leave. But his voice stopped her.

"Morganna—don't do this."

She paused, her back to him, her fingers brushing the edge of the book hidden beneath her cloak.

"I already have."

And then she was gone.

***

Later, as the Citadel grew quiet beneath the weight of another restless night, Morganna stood alone in her chambers, the forbidden book resting on her desk, its cover still cold to the touch.

She stared at it for a long time. Long enough for the candle to burn low, long enough for doubt to settle like dust around her.

Then—she opened it.

The pages shimmered with dark ink, symbols shifting beneath her gaze like living things. And written in the margins, scrawled in handwriting she didn't recognize, was a single line:

"This was never about saving the world." "It was always about saving you."

Her hands trembled. She didn't close the book.

And somewhere beyond the veil of reality— Kaelith smiled.

Chapter 12

"Grief is a strange companion. It does not demand your attention, yet it lingers. It does not speak, yet it whispers. And when it is quietest, that is when it is loudest of all."

Morganna sat cross-legged on the cold stone floor of her chambers, the forbidden book open before her. Candles flickered in a loose circle around her, their flames sputtering against the oppressive weight of the magic she was about to summon.

The ink on the pages didn't stay still. It writhed like veins under glass, shifting symbols that her mind should not have been able to comprehend— And yet, she did. She understood *too* easily.

"This was never about saving the world." "It was always about saving you."

Kaelith's whispered promise echoed through her mind, soft and seductive, threading through her thoughts like a dark melody.

She reached for the Weave. It felt different now—no longer the warm, golden current she had always known. The threads were thin, brittle, distant. But beneath them, deeper than she had ever dared reach before...

There was something else. A pulse. A shadow woven through the light. A place where the rules did not apply.

Morganna didn't hesitate. She dove into it.

Magic erupted around her in a burst of dark energy, the candle flames extinguished all at once, plunging the room into shadow. The symbols from the book lifted off the pages, twisting into the air, searing themselves into the stone floor like scars.

Pain hit her next—sharp and blinding. Like her veins were being unraveled from the inside out, her soul stretched too thin. But she didn't stop.

Because beneath the agony, she *felt* it— A thread. Familiar. Faint. *Him.*

Aeron.

Her breath hitched. She reached for it with everything she had left.

"Morganna."

His voice was clear this time, not a whisper, not an echo. *Real.*

But then—

The thread snapped. The magic collapsed. And Morganna screamed.

***

The room was quiet. Not the comforting kind of quiet that lulled you to sleep, but the brittle, suffocating kind that crept into the cracks of your thoughts and settled like dust in your lungs.

Rhylen sat hunched over a small, battered desk in the corner of his quarters, a flickering candle his only companion. The flame sputtered, casting long, restless shadows across the stone walls, stretching and shrinking like echoes of memories he couldn't outrun.

A half-empty bottle of something strong sat beside the stack of parchment—forgotten. His hands, rough from training, stained faintly with ink and old scars, trembled slightly as he pressed pen to paper.

Dear Aeron, I don't know why I'm doing this. You're not going to read it. You're not anywhere to read it. But I guess that's the point, isn't it?

He paused, staring at the words. They looked foreign the moment they left his mind, as if admitting them on paper made them real in a way thinking never could. His jaw clenched. He kept writing.

I should've stopped her. I should've saved you. I should've done something—anything—besides stand there like a gods-damned fool while the world fell apart around us.

His grip tightened around the pen until his knuckles whitened. The ink blotched slightly where his hand trembled, staining the parchment like a bruise.

You were reckless. You always were. Charging in like nothing could touch you, like fate was something you could punch in the face if it dared cross you. But it did, didn't it? It crossed you, and you left us. You left me.

He stopped, his breath hitching. The candle's flame bent in the draft sneaking through the cracks of the ancient stone, casting shadows that felt too much like ghosts.

Rhylen leaned back in his chair, staring at the ceiling, his eyes glassy but dry. He didn't cry anymore. Not because it didn't hurt—but because the grief had carved itself so deep there was nothing left to bleed.

After a moment, he dragged the pen back across the page.

She's gone, Aeron. Not dead, but gone all the same. And I don't know how to get her back.

His hand hovered, the pen trembling midair. Then he forced the words out.

But I think I can still reach her. Gods, it's like chasing a shadow, but there's something there. A flicker. A heartbeat that doesn't know it's still beating. She's buried under it all—rage, grief, whatever darkness Kaelith wrapped around her—but she's there. I know she is.

Rhylen stared at the ink as it dried, his heart pounding in his chest like it was trying to get out. He didn't know how long he sat there—long enough for the candle to burn low, wax dripping like the hours he'd never get back.

Eventually, he folded the letter. But instead of tucking it away like the others, he reached for a small metal dish sitting near the candle.

Inside it were ashes—bits of burnt parchment, crumpled remnants of letters he'd written before. Letters full of words that felt too heavy to keep but too painful to throw away.

Rhylen held the newest letter over the flame. The edges curled as the fire kissed the paper, turning white to black, black to nothing.

But when the flame licked closer to the center—to the part where he'd written *"I think I can still reach her"*— He pulled it back.

His hand trembled, breath ragged as he stared at the half-burnt letter. The words were scorched, edges fragile, but the heart of it remained. So did his hope. Thin. Frayed. But not gone.

With a shaky breath, Rhylen folded the half-burnt letter carefully and tucked it into the leather pouch he always carried. Right next to the small charm that had fallen from Morganna's bracelet years ago. A ghost of what was. A promise of what might still be.

When he finally lay down, staring at the ceiling again, the shadows didn't feel so empty.

***

Rhylen found her before anyone else did. He always did.

The door to her chambers was half-open, shadows bleeding from the gap like spilled ink. His instincts screamed at him to walk away, to leave her in peace— But he never listened to that voice. Not when it came to her.

He stepped inside. And froze.

The room was in ruins. The walls were scorched with marks he didn't recognize—symbols that pulsed faintly with dark energy. The forbidden book lay open on the floor, its pages torn and stained with something that looked far too much like blood.

And there, in the center of it all— Morganna.

She was on her knees, her hands buried in her hair, her body trembling. The shadows clung to her like a second skin, tendrils of darkness still coiling faintly around her fingertips.

"Morganna," Rhylen whispered, stepping forward.

She flinched, her head snapping up. Her eyes—once a brilliant violet—now flickered with streaks of black, like cracks in glass.

Rhylen's chest tightened. "What did you do?"

She didn't answer. Didn't have to.

Because he could feel it—the magic in the room. It was wrong. Twisted. It wasn't just that she'd used forbidden spells. She'd let them change her.

Rhylen crossed the room in three strides, dropping to his knees beside her. He reached out, his hand hovering over hers.

"Morganna," he said softly, "you're losing yourself."

She laughed. It was a broken sound, sharp and hollow.

"*I already have.*"

Rhylen's jaw clenched. His heart was screaming, but his voice stayed steady.

"No," he said quietly, "you're still here."

His fingers closed around hers. They were ice-cold. But she didn't pull away.

***

The days blurred after that. Morganna didn't stop. She couldn't.

She pushed deeper into the forbidden magic, each spell unraveling more of the person she used to be. The Weave no longer resisted her touch; it recoiled from it, as if recognizing the darkness threading through her soul.

Rhylen stayed. He trained beside her when she wanted to fight. He sat in silence when words were too much. And he watched—helpless—as she slipped further away.

One night, he found her standing alone in the Chamber of Threads.

The golden strands of fate flickered weakly around her, dimmer than he'd ever seen.

She turned when she heard him.

Her face was shadowed, her expression unreadable. But her eyes—Her eyes were burning with something he didn't recognize.

"Rhylen," she whispered, her voice softer than he'd ever heard it.

He swallowed hard. "Yeah?"

She hesitated, her fingers brushing over one of the threads, her touch light and reverent.

"If I brought him back..." she began, her voice trembling, "would you hate me for it?"

Rhylen felt like the ground had been ripped out from beneath him. His answer was soft. Painful. True.

"No." A beat. "But I'd be afraid for you."

Morganna didn't flinch. Didn't argue.

She just turned back to the Weave. And kept pulling.

***

Later that night, as Morganna sat alone with the forbidden book open in her lap, Kaelith's voice returned.

"You're close."

Her heart thudded painfully in her chest.

"Just a little more, Morganna. Reach further. Take what they said you couldn't."

Her fingers hovered over the page.

"You know where to find him."

She did. She always had.

And this time— She didn't hesitate.

Chapter 13

"The line between devotion and destruction is thinner than we care to admit. And when love becomes an obsession, even the brightest souls can be tempted by the dark."

Morganna sat cross-legged on the cold stone floor of her chambers, the forbidden book open before her. Candles flickered in a loose circle around her, their flames sputtering against the oppressive weight of the magic she was about to summon.

The ink on the pages didn't stay still. It writhed like veins under glass, shifting symbols that her mind should not have been able to comprehend—

And yet, she did. She understood *too* easily.

"*This was never about saving the world.*" "*It was always about saving you.*"

Kaelith's whispered promise echoed through her mind, soft and seductive, threading through her thoughts like a dark melody.

She reached for the Weave. It felt different now—no longer the warm, golden current she had always known. The threads were thin, brittle, distant. But beneath them, deeper than she had ever dared reach before...

There was something else. A pulse. A shadow woven through the light. A place where the rules did not apply.

Morganna didn't hesitate. She dove into it.

Magic erupted around her in a burst of dark energy, the candle flames extinguished all at once, plunging the room into shadow. The symbols from the book lifted off the pages, twisting into the air, searing themselves into the stone floor like scars.

Pain hit her next—sharp and blinding. Like her veins were being unraveled from the inside out, her soul stretched too thin. But she didn't stop.

Because beneath the agony, she *felt* it— A thread. Familiar. Faint. *Him.*

Aeron.

Her breath hitched. She reached for it with everything she had left.

"Morganna."

His voice was clear this time, not a whisper, not an echo. *Real.*

But then—

The thread snapped. The magic collapsed. And Morganna screamed.

***

Rhylen found her before anyone else did. He always did.

The door to her chambers was half-open, shadows bleeding from the gap like spilled ink. His instincts screamed at him to walk away, to leave her in peace— But he never listened to that voice. Not when it came to her.

He stepped inside. And froze.

The room was in ruins. The walls were scorched with marks he didn't recognize—symbols that pulsed faintly with dark energy. The forbidden book lay open on the floor, its pages torn and stained with something that looked far too much like blood.

And there, in the center of it all— Morganna.

She was on her knees, her hands buried in her hair, her body trembling. The shadows clung to her like a second skin, tendrils of darkness still coiling faintly around her fingertips.

"Morganna," Rhylen whispered, stepping forward.

She flinched, her head snapping up. Her eyes—once a brilliant violet—now flickered with streaks of black, like cracks in glass.

Rhylen's chest tightened. "What did you do?"

She didn't answer. Didn't have to.

Because he could feel it—the magic in the room. It was wrong. Twisted. It wasn't just that she'd used forbidden spells. She'd let them change her.

Rhylen crossed the room in three strides, dropping to his knees beside her. He reached out, his hand hovering over hers.

"Morganna," he said softly, "you're losing yourself."

She laughed. It was a broken sound, sharp and hollow.

I already have.

Rhylen's jaw clenched. His heart was screaming, but his voice stayed steady.

"No," he said quietly, "you're still here."

His fingers closed around hers. They were ice-cold. But she didn't pull away.

***

The days blurred after that. Morganna didn't stop. She couldn't.

She pushed deeper into the forbidden magic, each spell unraveling more of the person she used to be. The Weave no longer resisted her touch; it recoiled from it, as if recognizing the darkness threading through her soul.

Rhylen stayed. He trained beside her when she wanted to fight. He sat in silence when words were too much. And he watched—helpless—as she slipped further away.

One night, he found her standing alone in the Chamber of Threads.

The golden strands of fate flickered weakly around her, dimmer than he'd ever seen.

She turned when she heard him.

Her face was shadowed, her expression unreadable. But her eyes—Her eyes were burning with something he didn't recognize.

"Rhylen," she whispered, her voice softer than he'd ever heard it.

He swallowed hard. "Yeah?"

She hesitated, her fingers brushing over one of the threads, her touch light and reverent.

"If I brought him back..." she began, her voice trembling, "would you hate me for it?"

Rhylen felt like the ground had been ripped out from beneath him.

His answer was soft. Painful. True.

"No." A beat. "But I'd be afraid for you."

Morganna didn't flinch. Didn't argue.

She just turned back to the Weave. And kept pulling.

***

Later that night, as Morganna sat alone with the forbidden book open in her lap, Kaelith's voice returned.

"You're close."

Her heart thudded painfully in her chest.

"Just a little more, Morganna. Reach further. Take what they said you couldn't."

Her fingers hovered over the page.

"You know where to find him."

She did. She always had.

And this time— She didn't hesitate.

Chapter 14

"Grief is a doorway. Step through it, and you may find healing. Linger too long, and you may never find your way back."

The Book Was Cold.

Not the kind of cold that pricked the skin like frost or numbed the fingers like ice. This was different. The absence of warmth. Of meaning. A void pressed into the shape of a book.

Morganna's fingers hovered above it, trembling, her breath shallow as if the air itself had thinned. The runes etched into the cover pulsed faintly, dark veins of ink woven with threads she didn't recognize. They felt wrong beneath her touch. Not like ink. Not like magic. Like something alive. Like something *watching*.

"*Open it.*" The whisper slithered through her mind, soft as silk, sharp as glass. Kaelith didn't command. He didn't need to.

Because Morganna was already going to do it.

Her pulse roared in her ears as she lifted the cover, every part of her screaming to stop— But grief was louder. Grief was *always* louder.

The first page turned. And the world unraveled.

***

She didn't fall. She was *pulled*.

Dragged through the threads of reality like a needle stitching a new seam, her body folding through spaces that weren't meant to be crossed. The sensation was dizzying, like being caught between breaths, between heartbeats, between the fragile borders of existence itself.

When it stopped, she wasn't in the ruins anymore. The air was thicker here—heavy, electric, humming with an energy that wasn't the Weave but something older, something raw. Shadows stretched endlessly in every direction, stitched together with veins of violet light that pulsed like distant stars bleeding through the dark.

No ground. No sky. Just... existence.

And ahead— A figure stepped from the void.

Kaelith.

Not the fragment she'd fought before. Not the echo that had tried to devour the Heartstone.

This was his *true* form.

A silhouette woven from shadow and silence, his edges blurred like smoke caught in an unseen wind. His eyes—if they could be called that—were hollow voids, deep enough to drown galaxies.

He didn't speak at first. Didn't need to.

His presence filled the space like gravity, pressing against her chest until her next breath felt stolen.

But Morganna lifted her chin. Defiant. Dangerous. *Still Morganna.*

"I want to know how to bring him back."

Kaelith smiled. Not with lips—just with the way the darkness shifted around him, pleased, sharp, like a blade drawn slowly from its sheath.

"Of course you do."

***

Kaelith didn't offer power. Power was too crude. Too simple.

No, Kaelith offered something far more seductive: *Understanding*.

Because he knew. He had waited centuries for this. For a Guardian to question the Weave. For one to challenge fate itself. And Morganna—brilliant, grieving, defiant Morganna— She was *perfect*.

He circled her like a shadow stitched to her feet, his voice low and steady, curling around her thoughts like smoke and silk.

"You have felt him, haven't you?" She swallowed hard. Her throat was dry. "Yes."

A simple word. A fragile one. But it cracked something open inside her.

Kaelith's hollow eyes gleamed faintly. *"Then you know the truth."*

He drifted closer, though his feet never touched the ground. The space between them seemed to ripple, bending around him like even reality refused to get too close.

"The Weave did not erase him," he murmured. *"It bound him. A cruel trick of balance. A punishment dressed as sacrifice."*

Morganna's hands clenched into fists. Because she had *felt* it.

In the quiet moments when she touched the Weave. In the stolen whispers that echoed in her mind.

Aeron wasn't gone. He was *trapped*.

Kaelith's voice softened, patient, the way a snake might soothe its prey before striking. *"But fate is not absolute. The Weave can be undone. And you, Morganna—"* His shadows curled around her name like it belonged to him. *"—you were born to rewrite it."*

Her breath hitched. Because somewhere deep inside— She knew that was true.

She had always been different. Always been able to bend fate, to touch the threads of destiny in ways no other Guardian could.

And if she could change fate— Then she could bring Aeron back.

Kaelith saw the shift the moment she believed it. And his smile grew sharper.

"Come, little Guardian."

He lifted a hand.

A single thread unraveled from the darkness, floating between them—a fragile line of shadow, thin as silk, pulsing faintly.

"Let me show you how."

***

Morganna hesitated. Just for a moment.

She expected the Weave to resist her touch. Expected to feel pain, or rejection, or something that would tell her this was wrong.

But nothing happened.

The golden threads of fate didn't tighten around her magic. Didn't try to restrain her. Didn't *care*.

Instead—they yielded. Bent to her will like they always had.

Her heart raced. Her fingers trembled as she reached out, the dark thread drifting closer until it brushed against her skin.

She expected cold.

But it was *warm*. Alive.

A sharp breath shuddered through her.

This wasn't wrong. It wasn't corruption. It wasn't darkness.

It was just... understanding.

Her magic flared, not golden now, but a strange fusion of light and shadow, swirling together like ink bleeding into water. She twisted the thread between her fingers, weaving it without thought, without hesitation.

And the world responded.

A connection snapped into place— A tether stronger than fate. Stronger than death.

And deep in the Weave— *Something stirred.*

A voice. Distant. Faint.

"Morganna?"

Her heart slammed against her ribs. She gasped, her grip tightening on the thread.

"Aeron?"

It was him. Not a memory. Not an echo. *Him.*

Kaelith watched silently, his hollow gaze gleaming with triumph.

Because he knew. This was the moment. The moment she stopped fighting. The moment she realized the truth.

She could bring him back. She could undo fate.

And gods— She *would.*

***

Morganna's quarters were suffocatingly still. The faint glow of a dying hearth painted the stone walls in hues of gold and shadow, flickering like a heartbeat that refused to die. But there was no warmth left here—not in the cold stretch of the walls, not in the brittle air that pressed against her chest, and certainly not in her reflection.

She stood before the cracked mirror, its splintered glass a jagged tapestry of distorted fragments. Her face—her face—stared back in pieces, fractured like the world she'd tried to save. There were lines there she didn't remember earning, shadows hollowing the spaces beneath her once-bright eyes. Gold had faded from them, replaced by something darker, something restless.

She didn't recognize herself. Not anymore.

Her fingers—trembling, traitorous things—reached for the reflection, grazing the cold glass. A spiderweb of fractures fanned out from where her hand met its surface, thin veins of silver against the darkness. She pressed harder until the glass groaned beneath her touch, until the edges bit into her skin just enough to remind her she was still here.

Still here. When Aeron wasn't.

The memory ambushed her—unbidden, unwelcome.

Laughter. Bright, reckless, alive. Aeron's voice filling the training grounds, teasing her as she stumbled on purpose just to throw him off guard. *"You'll have to try harder than that, Morganna. Come on, show me the Guardian of Hope I keep hearing about."* The warmth of his hand catching hers when she did fall, the rough calluses of his fingers against her skin, grounding her, steadying her. *"You're not invincible, you know,"* he'd whispered once, brushing a stray lock of hair from her face. His smile had been soft, dangerous in the way it carved itself into places she hadn't known were vulnerable. *"And that's okay. That's what makes you real."*

She gasped like she'd been punched, staggering back from the mirror as if it had delivered the blow. The room spun, shadows lengthening, stretching toward her like fingers eager to claim what was left.

Her legs gave out, and she sank to the floor, her knees hitting the cold stone with a hollow thud. The bracelet on her wrist—the one Aeron had given her—caught the faint light, its charm tarnished but unbroken. She hated it for still being here. Hated herself for still wearing it.

Her chest ached, not with grief, but with something worse. Something hollow.

"You could have saved him."

The voice slithered through the silence, soft as silk, sharp as glass.

Morganna's head snapped up, her breath shallow. The room was empty, but the shadows pressed closer, coiling in the corners like they were listening.

"But you were too weak."

Her heart clenched. She knew that voice wasn't real. Except it was. Because it spoke the truth she couldn't escape.

She'd been too slow. Too blind. Too trusting. And Aeron had paid for it.

Her scream shattered the silence. She lunged for the mirror, fists clenched, magic burning beneath her skin—but she didn't use it. She didn't need it. She drove her hands into the glass, the shards exploding like frozen rain. Pain bloomed instantly, sharp and real, slicing through flesh, drawing crimson lines across her skin.

But she didn't stop. Couldn't.

She kept hitting until her knuckles were raw, until blood dripped from her fingertips, staining the stone like a fragile offering to a god that had never listened. When there was nothing left but broken glass and her ragged breathing, she collapsed, her hands trembling in her lap.

She stared at the blood. It felt... grounding. Real in a way nothing else did anymore.

The shadows shifted, drawn to her like moths to flame. They curled around her edges, whispering without voices, promising without words.

"You don't have to feel this," the darkness breathed, seeping into the cracks she'd left unguarded. *"You don't have to be weak."*

Morganna's fingers twitched. Blood dripped from the cuts, but she didn't heal them. She liked the sting. It was proof that something could still hurt.

She looked down at the bracelet again, the faint pulse of her magic tangled with it—Aeron's gift. His last piece of her. But he was gone. And she was still here.

Her voice was a whisper, rough and jagged as the glass around her. "I'll never be weak again."

The shadows stilled, listening. And then they answered.

Not with words. But with power.

It seeped into her like ink into water, dark and slow, filling the spaces Aeron had left behind. Her cuts closed—not with the warm, golden light of her old magic, but with something colder, something hollow.

Morganna didn't flinch. Didn't cry. Didn't mourn.

The world held its breath.

The darkness didn't move. The air was still. Even the Weave, for the first time in her life, was silent.

Like it, too, was waiting for what she would become.

She rose from the floor, leaving blood and broken glass behind. The light in her eyes was gone. In its place, something new burned.

Morgath was born.

***

Somewhere, across the Citadel, Rhylen woke with a sharp inhale, his chest tightening, his magic thrumming with something he couldn't explain.

A wrongness. A fracture.

Something had changed.

Chapter 15

"A soul does not break all at once. It fractures—piece by piece, thread by thread—until one day, there is nothing left to mend."

Rhylen Couldn't Save Aeron.

That truth had carved itself into his bones, lingering like a wound that refused to heal. Not fast enough. Not strong enough. Not enough.

But Morganna— He could still save her.

Because if there was one thing he knew with the certainty of every fractured piece of his heart— Aeron wouldn't have wanted this. Not for her. Not for the girl he loved.

And Rhylen had already lost too much to stand by and watch it happen again.

***

The Citadel's training grounds were silent, save for the hollow echo of footsteps on cracked stone. The torches lining the perimeter had long since burned out, leaving the vast space bathed in cold moonlight that spilled through fractured archways, casting jagged shadows like scars across the ground.

Rhylen stood at the center of the arena, alone.

His breath came in sharp bursts, fogging the night air as sweat clung to his skin despite the chill. His grip tightened around the hilt of his sword—an old, trusted weapon, its edge dulled from years of battles fought and lost. But tonight, he wasn't fighting a real enemy.

Tonight, he was fighting ghosts.

With a roar torn from somewhere deep in his chest, he lunged forward, slashing at nothing. His strikes were wild, unmeasured—a flurry of rage and regret, each swing carving through the air with reckless abandon. The blade sang with every strike, a hollow, brittle sound that didn't match the fury behind it.

He imagined Morganna standing before him, her eyes no longer warm gold but twisted violet, shadow coiling around her like armor. *Why didn't you stop her?* He swung harder. Faster. His muscles screamed, but he didn't care.

Then Aeron's face flashed in his mind. That easy grin, the fierce loyalty in his gaze. *You left me. You left us.* The sword crashed against the training dummy, splintering wood and sending shards flying. But it wasn't enough.

Rhylen's grip shifted, his knuckles white as he pivoted, now seeing his own reflection in the polished edge of the blade—a face carved with grief, with guilt, with failure. *You're the reason he's gone.* He struck again. And again. Until—

CRACK.

The blade shattered mid-swing, fragments scattering across the stone like broken pieces of a life he couldn't put back together. Rhylen stumbled forward, breath ragged, falling to his knees. The hilt remained clenched in his trembling hands, jagged metal where the blade had once been whole.

Silence settled again.

He stared at the ruined weapon, chest heaving, heart pounding against ribs that felt too fragile to hold it all in. His fingers tightened around the broken hilt until his skin split, blood dripping onto the stone. But he didn't care. He welcomed the sting.

Lowering his head, his forehead pressed against the cool earth, Rhylen's voice came out a shattered whisper—soft, fragile, like the blade in his hands.

"I'll fix this. I'll fix you."

But he didn't know if he was talking to the sword. Or to Aeron. Or to Morganna. Or to himself.

***

A clearing outside the Citadel, just after a grueling mission. The night is cool, the fire crackling softly. Shadows dance on the trees, flickering like the ghosts of battles already fading.

Rhylen leans back against a fallen log, exhaustion settling into his bones. His sword lies discarded nearby, nicked and dirt-smeared from the fight. Morganna sits opposite him, her knees drawn to her chest, eyes reflecting the fire's glow. Between them, Aeron tends to the flames, his grin as bright as the embers sparking into the night.

"Did you see Rhylen's face when that wyrm lunged at him?" Aeron teases, tossing a small twig into the flames. "I swear, he nearly tripped over his own dignity."

Rhylen rolls his eyes, but a crooked smile betrays him. "I was *strategically repositioning*."

"Oh, is that what we're calling running for your life now?" Aeron laughs, the sound full and warm, the kind of laugh that burrows into your chest and stays there.

Morganna snorts softly, shaking her head. "He's got a point, Rhy. That wasn't exactly graceful."

Rhylen throws a small stone toward her—missing on purpose. "Traitor."

The fire crackles, filling the comfortable silence that settles between them. Aeron leans back on his elbows, staring up at the sky where stars pierce the darkness like distant sparks of hope.

Rhylen's gaze drifts, not to the stars, but to Morganna.

She's not laughing anymore, though a faint smile lingers. Her eyes aren't on the fire—they're on Aeron. Soft. Unspoken. A thousand words unsaid, tucked behind a glance.

And Rhylen feels it—the ache of something fragile and fierce all at once. Not jealousy. Just... knowing.

Knowing that no matter how many battles they fight, how many victories they claim, Aeron is the gravity they both orbit.

Now, Rhylen lays alone by another fire, older now, the warmth unable to touch the cold lodged deep in his chest. His sword lies beside him, polished but useless against the kind of battles he fights now—the ones in his head.

The laughter is gone. The fire crackles the same way. But it feels hollow without them.

He stares into the flames, as if looking hard enough might pull that memory back in full. But it doesn't.

***

Kaelith stood at the edge of the Veil, where the worlds thinned, his form shifting between solid and shadow as he watched Rhylen move through the ruins below.

The Guardian was relentless. Bloodied, exhausted, driven by something Kaelith found endlessly amusing.

Love.

It was such a foolish thing—so breakable, so malleable.

And yet, Rhylen clung to it. Let it shape him, let it fuel him, let it burn him.

Kaelith's lips curled in amusement as Rhylen's magic flared in the darkness, a sharp contrast to the creeping void that had claimed these lands. He wasn't like Morganna—not yet. He still carried the light, even if it flickered.

"But for how long?"

Kaelith could stop him. Could send his shadows to swallow Rhylen whole, end his pathetic hunt before it began.

But where was the fun in that?

Instead, he lifted a hand—and the shadows shifted, ever so slightly.

A path cleared. A whisper of guidance.

Not to save Rhylen.

But to test Morganna.

"What will you do, little queen?" Kaelith mused, watching Rhylen push forward, oblivious to the unseen hand guiding him.

"Will you still choose him?"

The thought entertained him.

And so he let Rhylen find her.

***

The Citadel wasn't crumbling from stone and shadow. It was crumbling from within.

The Weave frayed at the edges, strands unraveling like forgotten threads in an ancient tapestry. The Heartstone pulsed weakly, flickering as though mourning its own brokenness.

At the center of it all— Morganna.

No. Not Morganna. Morgath.

Rhylen had felt the shift when she crossed that invisible line, when grief turned to rage, and love curdled into something sharp enough to wound the world. But he refused to believe she was gone.

Not yet.

So he followed her trail, through ruins swallowed by shadow, across desolate lands where the Weave no longer sang, into places the Guardians had sworn never to set foot.

And with every step, her darkness grew stronger. And his resolve grew sharper.

***

Morganna's throne room, the shadows thick and oppressive, Kaelith's voice a distant whisper. The bracelet pulses faintly, like a heartbeat she refuses to acknowledge.

Across realms, Rhylen sits by another dying fire, staring into the flames as if he can see her through them.

Both of them reach for the same ghost in different ways— Morganna gripping the bracelet. Rhylen holding a burnt letter.

Both believing they're the only ones left remembering.

But the memory holds them both. Tethered. Fractured. Still connected.

***

The first clue waited in the ruins of Aeryon's Hollow, once a sacred site woven tightly with the early threads of the Weave. Now it was nothing but ash and ruin.

At the center of the destruction, carved with precision and fury, was a mark: Morganna's sigil—distorted, darkened, twisted into something unrecognizable.

A message.

Not a warning. A challenge.

She wanted him to find her.

***

After days of pursuit, bloodied from battles with shadows she left in her wake, Rhylen collapsed beneath a fractured archway, staring at the sky—a canvas torn by cracks of violet light.

His breath came ragged, sharp with ash and exhaustion. But it wasn't the bruises that hurt most. It was her.

Morganna was gone. Not in body, but in every other way that mattered.

Rhylen's hand drifted to his pocket, fingers brushing something small—cold and familiar. When he pulled it free, his heart clenched.

A charm.

Battered. Frayed at the edges. Once part of Morganna's bracelet—the one Aeron had given her. The one she'd always worn like a heartbeat stitched to her skin.

But somewhere along the way, she'd lost this piece. Or maybe— She'd thrown it away.

Rhylen's fingers tightened around it. His chest ached like it might shatter from the weight of everything unsaid.

His voice was a whisper, raw and fragile. "I won't fail her too."

The words disappeared into the fractured sky. But the promise stayed.

***

When he finally found her, it was at the ruins of the Forgotten Spire, where the Weave's original threads had once been anchored. Now, the land itself was sick—twisted, pulsing with veins of shadow.

And there she was. Standing at the edge of a broken altar, shadows coiling around her like armor.

"Morganna," he whispered, her name tasting like both prayer and curse.

She turned slowly. And her eyes— Gods, her eyes— Were not hers anymore.

Violet streaked with black veins of magic. A gaze that didn't see him— Only what stood in her way.

***

The battle wasn't with blades. It never was.

It was with words.

"Morganna," Rhylen rasped, blood seeping from wounds he no longer felt, his breath ragged but unbroken. "You can't bring him back."

She flinched. A small crack.

Her magic surged anyway, lashing out like a living thing. It hit him with the force of a dying star, sending him sprawling, his body broken against the altar's shattered steps.

But he got up. He always did.

Blood dripped from the corner of his mouth. His knees trembled. But his voice— His voice stayed steady.

"If you're gone," he whispered, "then so am I."

She hesitated. Just for a heartbeat. Just long enough.

Rhylen collapsed beside her, one hand clutching the charm, his heart thundering with everything he couldn't say. His fingers trembled as he reached for her wrist, pressing the charm against the bracelet still wrapped there.

And with his last breath— He wove.

***

The magic wasn't grand. It wasn't a burst of light or a roar of power.

It was a whisper. A thread stitched from the fragments of three souls.

Rhylen poured the last sliver of himself into the bracelet—a fragile, defiant piece of his soul—binding it to the charm, to Morganna's light, to Aeron's love.

The moment it fused, he felt it. Aeron's voice, faint but steady. Morganna's laugh, distant but real.

Memories surged— Sunlight on stone steps. Laughter in forbidden places. A family made, not born.

Tears blurred his vision. His heart faltered. But his hope didn't.

"Come back to us," he whispered. And then— He was gone.

***

The bracelet snapped into place on Morgath's wrist—seamless, eternal.

She screamed. Morganna's scream tore through the night as the magic wrapped around her wrist, fusing the bracelet into place.

She clawed at it—**shadows flaring from her fingertips, magic unraveling reality itself—**but the silver threads held.

Unbroken.

Unyielding.

Then—the visions came.

Aeron's laugh, sharp and golden, echoing through the training grounds.

Rhylen's smirk, the way his voice grumbled with irritation when she bested him in a duel.

The firelit nights—the quiet ones—where they weren't warriors, weren't Guardians, just three people who belonged to each other in a way the world could never take away.

"Morganna," Aeron whispered, *his voice warm, real—too real.*

Her breath hitched.

She felt his hand on hers.

Felt Rhylen's steady presence at her back.

For just a moment—**one fragile, aching moment—**she was herself again.

The shadows recoiled.

Her magic stuttered.

"No—"

The word was a raw, fractured sound. A plea. A denial.

Then—she crushed it.

Crushed the feeling, the memories, the weakness.

With a snarl, she wrenched herself free—not from the bracelet, but from the moment.

Her violet eyes flared, shadow consuming the flicker of gold that had threatened to return.

"No more."

Her magic surged, and the visions were gone.

Aeron was gone.

Rhylen was gone.

And Morganna was gone too.

Only Morgath remained.

***

Morganna wanted to see it only as a bracelet, however, it wasn't just a bracelet. It was Aeron's love, Morganna's light, and Rhylen's hope—woven into something eternal.

No matter how far she fell. No matter how dark she became.

It would always return to her. It would never let her forget.

***

Reality fractured around her, the Weave retreating, the light too fragile to fight anymore. Morgath stood in the ruins of what had been a world.

Kaelith approached, his voice soft as silk. "You are more than a Guardian now," he whispered. "You are a queen."

She didn't respond. She couldn't.

Because on her wrist— Hope still burned.

And deep inside, beneath layers of grief and shadow— Morganna was still there.

Waiting.

Chapter 16

"The cruelest victories are not won with blades, but with whispers. Let them believe they have chosen the darkness—until they can no longer remember the light."

The corruption did not spread all at once.

Like Morgath herself, it was patient.

It crept, slow and insidious, weaving through the cracks left behind by the shattered Heartstone—a shadow stitched into the very fabric of Elysoria. The first lands to fall were not taken by force. No armies marched. No banners burned.

Instead, it began with whispers. A chill in the wind where warmth once lingered. Forests grew darker, ancient trees twisting into unfamiliar shapes, their branches clawing at the sky as if recoiling from the light they once cradled. Rivers ran colder, their waters blackened with veins of shadow, reflecting not the sky but something darker beneath the surface. The heavens themselves dimmed—not quite as bright, not quite as vast—as if the stars were slowly forgetting how to shine.

It was subtle at first. Until it wasn't.

***

Morgath stood at the highest peak of the Shadow Realm, her violet eyes scanning the land below—her kingdom of ruin.

The darkness stretched as far as she could see. The Weave had unraveled beneath her hand, and yet—something itched beneath her skin. A faint flicker. A whisper of a self that should no longer exist.

"Morganna."

The name slid into her thoughts like a knife between ribs.

Her breath caught—just for a moment.

And that was when Kaelith stepped in.

His presence curled around her mind like smoke, his voice velvet-soft, careful. Dangerous.

"You hesitate, my queen."

Morgath straightened, her jaw tightening. "No."

The flicker was gone. Burned away.

Kaelith moved closer—not touching her, but near enough that she felt his presence pressing in, guiding, directing. "The Weave resists you still," he murmured, his voice laced with amusement. "It is afraid. The prophecy speaks of your triumph, does it not?"

Morgath turned to him sharply. "The prophecy—"

Kaelith lifted a hand—a flick of the wrist, a twist of power. Shadows thickened around them, swallowing the weak light that dared to remain. His expression did not shift, but his voice was careful. Precise.

"When shadows rise and the dragon wakes, twelve hearts entwined the darkness break."

He let the words settle. Then, smoothly, he twisted them.

"They fear you, my queen. The Fated Twelve—the last desperate flailings of a world that refuses to kneel." His hollow gaze locked onto hers, an abyss drawing her deeper. "But fate does not belong to them." He let the shadows pulse beneath his fingertips. "You are the darkness that rises. You are the prophecy's end."

Morgath exhaled slowly.

Kaelith's magic wove through her thoughts like silk, erasing doubt before it could fester.

Yes.

She was not the villain in this tale.

She was its reckoning.

***

The world forgot itself, piece by piece.

Not all at once. That would have been too easy.

No, the unraveling was slow. Insidious.

The sky above the once-bright city of Eldershade dimmed—not to night, but to something worse. An eternal dusk that never truly faded, never truly brightened.

In the streets, an old woman looked up at the heavens, her eyes narrowing. Her lips parted, her fingers twitching at her side.

And then—her face twisted in confusion.

"What... was it?" she murmured.

Her daughter turned to her, frowning. "What was what?"

"The sky," the old woman whispered, voice uncertain. "It used to—" She hesitated, her mouth opening and closing.

She couldn't remember.

Farther down the street, a child chased after his own shadow, laughing—until it stretched.

Too long.

Too sharp.

The laughter died on his lips.

The shadow twisted, reaching back toward him.

He screamed.

The mother ran to him, clutching his shoulders. "It's fine, love," she said, but her voice shook.

The child only stared at the ground, his small hands trembling. "It wasn't mine," he whispered.

And in a distant valley, where the rivers once ran silver, the waters blackened.

A merchant knelt by the edge, cupping a handful to his lips before freezing. The reflection staring back at him was not his own.

It smiled.

The world was forgetting itself.

And Morgath did not care.

***

Morgath stood on the battlefield, her enemies broken before her. The Weave's remnants frayed at the edges, unable to resist the force of her will.

Another city fallen. Another kingdom shattered beneath the weight of her power.

The Guardians had fought, of course. They always did. But their light had flickered out, one by one.

She lifted her hand, shadow curling around her fingertips as she reached for the last ember of resistance—the last soldier who dared to stand.

Their eyes met.

Golden.

Defiant.

For a heartbeat, something in her stirred.

Then—she struck.

The warrior crumpled, their magic snuffed out like a dying star.

She straightened, turning to Kaelith, expecting approval—but his eyes were not on her.

He was staring at her wrist.

Morgath frowned, following his gaze.

The bracelet.

It was... warm.

Not hot. Not burning.

But warm.

The charm pulsed—just for a second. A soft, rhythmic beat.

Like a heart.

Like a breath.

Like defiance.

A flicker of unease whispered beneath her ribs.

No.

No.

Morgath curled her fingers into a fist, shadows surging to smother the warmth.

It was nothing.

It meant nothing.

The battle was won.

She had won.

And yet—

As Kaelith watched her, his amusement flickered.

Because he had seen it.

He had seen the moment Morganna flickered through.

And though Morgath did not look at him, she felt his shadows tighten ever so slightly around her mind.

"Careful, my queen."

She was his.

She would stay his.

No matter how many times the bracelet pulsed.

No matter how many times it refused to forget.

***

She did not need armies. She needed souls. Fractured ones. The kind that bled easily when you pressed on the right wound.

And she had found them.

The Wolf King - Once a proud leader of the Moonspire Clans, he had been a creature of honor, his voice a hymn sung beneath silver skies. Now, he was something else. Half-beast, half-man. A crown rusted by betrayal fused into twisted horns, his eyes pale as the moon he once worshiped, but hollow where light used to live. His kingdom had been torn from him, his people scattered like ash on the wind.

Morgath did not offer him a crown. She offered him a pack. A kingdom carved from fear and loyalty sharper than any blade. And he howled her name into the night, his voice a promise wrapped in hunger and rage.

But sometimes—just sometimes—when the moon was full, his howl fractured, a note of sorrow tangled in the fury.

Lord Malachor - A fallen noble whose name was once spoken with reverence, now nothing more than a curse. His armor, once pristine and gleaming with sigils of light, was tarnished and cracked, a reflection of the man within. His lands had been the first to wither under Morgath's influence—not burned, but rotted from within, like fruit left too long in the dark.

Morgath did not offer him redemption. She offered him vengeance. A blade forged from his own hatred, sharpened on the memory of every betrayal he had ever suffered. And he wielded it gladly.

But when his reflection caught in broken glass, he sometimes flinched—because he did not recognize the face that stared back.

Duke Varek - A warlord who had once fought for the Light—and lost everything. His sword had once sworn oaths to the Weave, etched with runes of protection and honor. Now, those runes were scarred over, burned black by the void magic that had replaced his faith.

Morgath did not offer him purpose. She offered him freedom. The freedom to take, to destroy, to carve his own path without the burden of oaths he could no longer believe in. And he followed her into the dark, his sword no longer bound by promises—only by power.

Yet, when he passed old battlegrounds, where fallen comrades' names were carved into stone, his grip tightened on the hilt—not out of rage, but memory.

***

Morgath's champions did not wear her sigil. They did not need to.

Their existence was her banner. Their victories were her sermons. Their brokenness was her masterpiece.

As their influence spread, kingdoms crumbled—not from invasion, but from within. Corruption seeded itself in whispered promises:

- *"You deserve more."*

- *"They betrayed you."*

- *"I can give you what they took."*

Morgath didn't have to conquer. She only had to offer.

***

But even as her darkness rippled across Elysoria, a faint thread of something unsettled tugged at the edges of her awareness. Not fear. Not doubt. Something else.

A memory buried deep beneath the layers of shadow she had wrapped around herself. A flicker she couldn't kill. A warmth she couldn't smother.

The bracelet pulsed against her wrist. She ignored it. She always did.

But the sensation lingered—like a heartbeat that wasn't hers.

A prophecy long buried, forgotten even by the Guardians who once guarded it, surfaced in the recesses of her mind.

"When shadows rise and the dragon wakes, Twelve hearts entwined the darkness break."

Morgath's lips curled into a cold smile. Let them rise. She would break them long before they ever reached her.

And when the last of the Fated Twelve had fallen, there would be nothing left to stop her from rewriting the world in her image. Not the Weave. Not the Light. Not even fate itself.

But far beneath the layers of shadow and grief, deep within her soul— The bracelet remained. Anchored. Undestroyed.

And Morganna was still there. Buried. Broken. Waiting.

Chapter 17

"The past is a stubborn thing. Bury it, burn it, break it—still, it lingers, whispering in the spaces between heartbeats."

Morgath stood at the edge of the Shadow Realm, where the sky was a hollow canvas, void of stars, smeared with tendrils of black mist that slithered like dying echoes. Below her, Elysoria stretched in distant fragments—a fractured tapestry woven with threads of light she'd long since unraveled.

But beyond the darkness, nestled like an ember refusing to die, there was a faint glow. The Heartstone.

Even now—even broken—it still existed. It should have infuriated her. It should have made her rage burn hotter than the void she had become.

Instead— It *called* to her.

Not with words. Not with magic. But with something worse. A faint echo of a heartbeat she could no longer feel in her own chest. A fragile pulse that mimicked the rhythm of what her heart had forgotten.

Her fingers twitched, curling into fists as if trying to grasp something that wasn't there. And beneath the shadow-wrought fabric of her sleeve— The bracelet pulsed.

She froze. It wasn't the faint hum she'd grown used to ignoring. No. This was stronger. A steady thrum, rhythmic and deliberate, beating in time with—

Her heart.

Morgath's breath hitched. She yanked back her sleeve, revealing the silver-threaded bracelet—the one Aeron had given her, the one that refused to be broken, burned, or lost. Its simple charm glimmered faintly, untouched by the corruption etched into her skin. And it pulsed. Not with shadow. But with light.

Her voice was barely a whisper, a breath of memory woven into sound. "Aeron."

Nothing. No answer. No whisper in the Weave. No warmth in the magic she'd once cradled like a lifeline.

Just the pulse. Relentless. Inescapable.

***

"He is lost to you."

Kaelith's voice slithered into her mind, a serpent coiling through the cracks of her grief, soft and suffocating. He wasn't beside her. He didn't need to be. His presence was stitched into the very shadows that clung to her—a parasite with velvet words.

Morgath's jaw clenched, her violet eyes narrowing as the bracelet's pulse quickened. No. *She refused to believe that.* The Weave had taken Aeron from her. Fate had carved him from her ribs like he was never meant to stay.

But if she could unravel fate once— She could do it again.

Her hand shot to the bracelet, fingers clawing at it, trying to tear it free. It didn't budge. It never did.

A burst of shadow magic flared from her fingertips, but the bracelet remained untouched, its silver threads gleaming defiantly against the dark veins creeping beneath her skin. It pulsed harder—like it was fighting her. Or fighting *for* her.

She let out a snarl, turning away from the Heartstone's distant glow, trying to drown out the rhythm that wouldn't stop. *Ba-dum. Ba-dum. Ba-dum.* Her heartbeat. Not the void's. *Hers.*

***

Morganna and Aeron sit atop the rooftop of the Citadel, in the late afternoon. The sky is streaked with gold and pink, the sun sinking low. They sit side by side, legs dangling over the ledge, a rare moment of peace after weeks of relentless training.

Aeron holds a small charm in his fingers—a simple star etched into a piece of silver. His hands are rough from battles, but gentle as he braids it into the leather bracelet on Morganna's wrist.

Morganna watches him, pretending not to care, but her heart beats faster with every twist of the leather.

"You know," Aeron says softly, fingers still working, "this isn't for luck."

Morganna arches a brow. "No?"

He glances at her, a grin tugging at the corner of his mouth—but his eyes are serious. "It's for you to remember who you are when things get dark."

She doesn't reply right away, afraid her voice might betray the storm brewing in her chest.

Instead, she looks down at the charm as he ties the final knot, securing it in place. His fingers brush her skin—just for a second, but it feels like forever.

Aeron leans back on his hands, satisfied. "There. Now, no matter what happens, you'll always find your way back."

Morganna forces a smirk, trying to keep it light. "What if I don't get lost?"

His smile softens, eyes meeting hers. "You will. Everyone does."

Today, Morganna stands alone in the heart of her shadow-forged kingdom, the silver bracelet still wrapped around her wrist, with the same star charm. The charm glints faintly, dulled by time but untouched by her darkness.

Her fingers trace it absentmindedly—shadow-streaked, black veins threading up her arms like cracks in stone.

She squeezes the bracelet until her knuckles turn white, as if she could crush the memory along with it.

But it won't break.

It never does.

***

Her eyes snapped open, burning with violet fire, threaded with veins of shadow that pulsed in time with that infernal, fragile beat. The Heartstone still existed. And as long as it did—so did Aeron.

Maybe not in the way she remembered. Maybe not in the way she wanted. But somewhere in that fragile shard of light was the piece of him she refused to lose.

If she couldn't find him— She would remake him. *If the Weave wouldn't return him—* She would tear it apart, thread by thread, until it begged her to stop.

She would rebuild the Heartstone in her own image. Not as a symbol of balance. Not as a beacon of light. But as a monument to everything she'd lost— And everything she was willing to destroy to get it back.

Her magic surged, dark tendrils weaving into the sky, pulling at the fragile threads of reality itself. The ground beneath her feet cracked, veins of shadow spiraling outward, a reflection of the fractures inside her own soul.

But the bracelet kept pulsing. Steady. Defiant. A heartbeat she couldn't silence.

***

A bitter wind from the Shadow Realm tugged at her cloak, cold and hollow, but she felt none of its chill. Only the distant warmth of the Heartstone—faint, infuriatingly alive.

She hated it. She needed it.

Because as long as that flickering light remained, so did the chance to rewrite everything.

And when she did— She would tear the Weave apart. She would unmake the stars if she had to. She would burn the world down to its last breath.

And she would take back what had been stolen from her. No matter what it cost.

The bracelet's pulse slowed—matching the rhythm of her rage, her grief, her shadowed heart. But it didn't stop. It never would.

Because hidden beneath the darkness, buried deep where even she couldn't reach— Morganna was still there. A flicker. A fracture. A final glimpse of light.

***

Morgath found herself in a dreamscape—still, silent, untouched by shadow. The lake where Morganna and Aeron once found a rare moment of peace. The water glistens under a soft, golden sky, reflecting clouds tinged with pink and orange, untouched by darkness. Gentle ripples lap at the shore, the breeze carrying the faint scent of wildflowers, sweet and familiar.

She stands at the edge of the lake, barefoot. She doesn't remember walking here. The cold bite of Shadowfell's endless dark is gone, replaced by warmth that settles against her skin like an old memory. She frowns, her eyes narrowing. This isn't real. It *can't* be real.

But it *feels* real.

The breeze shifts, and with it— His voice.

Soft. Warm. Familiar.

"You're late."

She turns sharply.

Aeron stands a few steps away, the sun catching in his hair, his crooked smile carved into her memory exactly as she left it. No shadow clings to him, no mark of death, no echo of the loss she's wrapped herself in like armor.

Just him. As he was.

Alive.

Morgath's breath catches in her throat, fury rising fast to choke the ache beneath it. Her magic flares instinctively—a pulse of violet shadow coiling around her fingertips, dark and lethal.

But nothing happens.

The magic fizzles, useless, like striking flint against wet stone.

Aeron doesn't flinch. He steps closer, his gaze soft, head tilted slightly as if he's trying to see through her.

Through Morgath. Back to Morganna.

"Is this what you wanted?" he asks gently, like they're still back in the Citadel gardens, arguing over reckless plans and unspoken feelings.

Her hands curl into fists. "You're not real."

He doesn't deny it. Just watches her with that infuriating, knowing look—the one that always made her feel seen, even when she didn't want to be.

Morgath lunges, shadowfire erupting from her palms, jagged and furious. The dreamscape should shatter under the force of it. *He* should shatter.

But nothing burns.

The fire dies before it reaches him, leaving only the echo of her ragged breath.

Aeron steps closer. No fear. No hesitation.

He holds out his hand, palm up. Resting there is a charm—A intricately woven knot, delicate and simple, snug between a braided silver thread. The very charm he once gave her, long before the shadows claimed her heart.

"For protection," he'd said back then, fastening it around her wrist with fingers that brushed her skin like a promise. "It's tied to my magic. A little extra strength when you need it."

She'd worn it like armor. She'd torn it off when he died.

But here it is again, gleaming softly, untouched by time or grief.

Morgath snarls, striking out again—not with magic this time, but with her bare hands, desperate to tear the vision apart, to feel *something* real beneath her fingertips.

Her hand passes through him like mist.

Aeron's expression doesn't change. He closes his fingers around the charm, lowering his hand. "You can't kill me," he murmurs. "I'm not the shadow you're fighting."

She staggers back, breath ragged, her fury crumbling under the weight of something colder.

Because he's right. She can't kill him. Not here. Not anywhere.

The world around her begins to ripple, the dream fraying at the edges like a thread pulled too tight.

His voice follows her as she's pulled back into waking. Soft. Steady. Unforgiving.

"Is this what you wanted? Morganna, I am still here.'"

Morgath jolts awake.

Darkness wraps around her again, the cold, familiar emptiness of the Shadow Realm pressing in. Her chest heaves with breaths she can't steady. Her hands tremble, clutching something—

She looks down.

The bracelet.

Its silver threads glint faintly, the charm nestled against her palm. She doesn't remember reaching for it. Doesn't remember holding it so tightly that her nails have left crescent marks in her skin.

She snarls, yanking at it, trying to tear it from her wrist. The shadows obey every command she's ever given—except this one.

The bracelet holds.

Stubborn. Unyielding. Like him.

Morgath shoves herself to her feet, fury burning hot enough to drown out the ache she can't seem to kill.

She will not be haunted. She will not be broken.
But her hand won't let go.

Chapter 18

"Even the deepest shadows cannot erase what is written in the soul. Love, loss, and fate—they do not end. They wait." The Shadow Realm was silent. Not the quiet of peace, nor the stillness of sleep, but the kind of silence that settled over a place forgotten by the living—a silence that didn't wait to be broken because it had never been whole to begin with.

The air was heavy, thick with magic, yet lifeless—just as Morgath had intended it to be.

Darkness pulsed through the blackened stone of her throne chamber, veins of shadow rippling like blood beneath cracked obsidian. The ceiling stretched high into a void of endless night, where the stars had long since been devoured, leaving only the faint echo of light that dared not return. The floor was etched with remnants of the Weave—fractured threads, splintered runes—faint reminders of what she had destroyed and what she still sought to unmake.

At the center of it all, Morgath sat in silence, her hands resting lightly against the jagged arms of her throne. The throne itself was carved from the remains of fallen Guardians, a twisted monument to everything she had lost—and everything she had claimed in return.

The shadows bent around her like servants, curling in deference, in fear. But even shadows could not mask the truth. She was haunted. Not by ghosts. By memory.

The void hissed in displeasure, a thin thread of mockery woven into the darkness.

"You mourn him still," it taunted, coiling through the cracks in her mind like cold breath against her skin. *"Even now. Even after all you have done."*

Morgath's hands tightened on the throne. Her nails bit into her palms, sharp enough to break the skin, but she welcomed the pain. It was the only thing that still felt real—the only thing that reminded her she was still here.

When he was not.

"I do not mourn," she whispered, her voice a blade drawn from its sheath.

She did not. She would not. Grief was for those too weak to change what had been lost.

And Morgath had no use for grief. Not when she could still bring him back.

The golden past-self—the naïve, broken girl clutching a dead man's memory—was gone, buried beneath layers of shadow and fury. She had carved that part of herself out like rot from a wound, leaving only the raw edges of ambition and rage.

But even now, when the world trembled beneath her feet, when kingdoms fell with a flick of her hand— Aeron's voice still haunted her.

It wasn't real. It couldn't be. And yet—she heard him.

"You see fate as a thing to shape," he had once whispered, teasing, his hands tangled in her hair, his smile the kind of warmth that made the stars jealous. They had stood beneath an unbroken sky, the Weave humming around them like a song only they knew. *"But some things are simply meant to be, my love."*

She had laughed then— Drunk on love and moonlight. Drunk on the foolish belief that nothing could touch them.

"And some things are meant to be undone," she had replied, her words light, careless, never realizing how deep they would one day cut.

She had not understood what those words would mean. Not until she had lost him. Not until she had watched the Weave take him from her, indifferent and merciless, uncaring that she had loved him more than life itself.

She should have been strong enough to save him. She should have been everything fate feared.

Instead— She had wept.

She had fallen to her knees before the Heartstone, her tears mingling with blood and ash, begging for another path, another way, another chance.

But the Light had only whispered its cruel song: *"This was always meant to be."*

Her nails scraped against the arm of her throne, leaving deep grooves in the stone. Her reflection flickered in the fractured obsidian like a ghost of the girl she had once been.

"I was meant to be the Guardian of Hope."

That's what Aeron had called her, once. His voice full of devotion, full of love. Full of lies.

Because love had failed her. Hope had abandoned her. And the only thing strong enough to change fate was her own hand.

If hope would not bring him back— Then she would rewrite the world without it.

***

Morgath rose from her throne, her shadow stretching across the vast chamber, long and sharp like the blade she no longer needed to carry. Her magic was enough—a pulse of void stitched into her very soul.

Kaelith appeared from the darkness, his form coalescing like smoke given shape, his hollow eyes gleaming with approval.

"The world bends beneath you, my queen," he said softly, his voice a velvet poison. *"And still, you are restless."*

Morgath's jaw tightened.

She hated that he was right. Because power wasn't enough. Not when it couldn't bring Aeron back.

"The Weave still resists," Kaelith continued, stepping closer. *"Its remnants scattered, hiding in the hearts of the weak. But they will fall, one by one. And when the last thread is cut—"*

"I will find him," Morgath finished, her voice cold and certain. *"I will tear apart every soul, every realm, until there is nowhere left for him to hide."*

Kaelith smiled. But his gaze flicked briefly—almost imperceptibly—to the bracelet on her wrist, where a faint, defiant glow pulsed like a heartbeat.

His smile didn't falter. But it didn't reach his eyes.

"Then we begin again."

***

She stood on the balcony of her citadel, gazing out at the fractured horizon. The lands of Elysoria stretched far beyond, their skies dimmed, their rivers choked with the ash of forgotten gods.

But there was still light. Still resistance. Not for long.

Morgath lifted her hand, her bracelet glinting faintly in the darkness—the charm, tarnished but unbroken, bound to her wrist by the last fragile thread of who she had been.

She would unravel that too. Eventually.

For now, she had work to do.

"Let the world grieve," she whispered, her magic spilling from her fingertips like ink in water. *"Let the light remember what it means to be afraid."*

A curse bloomed from her hands, dark as the void itself, spreading like wildfire across the remnants of the Weave—twisting, consuming, corrupting.

Forests withered. Oceans boiled. Stars blinked out, one by one.

The first of many.

And as the world screamed, Morgath listened— Waiting for the only voice that mattered to call her back.

But the silence remained. And so did she.

***

Morgath returned to her throne, her steps soundless against the fractured stone, her magic trailing behind her like a shadow that had forgotten how to detach.

She sat. And the bracelet pulsed.

Not with darkness. Not with void.

With warmth.

A heartbeat she could not claim as her own, steady and defiant against the hollow vastness inside her.

She clenched her fist, willing the pulse to stop, to fade, to *die*. But it remained. A fragile ember refusing to be snuffed out.

She had tried to be rid of it. She had thrown it into the abyss. Burned it with shadowfire. Crushed it beneath magic that had unraveled kingdoms.

And yet— It always returned, the longest it was gone was a day. That was when she had burned it with shadow fire and tossed it into the abyss. She awoke the next day with it wrapped around her wrist as pristine as the day Aeron had placed it there.

Morgath's breath shuddered through clenched teeth.

It was not just a bracelet. It was a chain. A reminder.

Of love. Of light. Of the girl she had been.

"I do not mourn," she whispered again, her voice brittle this time.

But the bracelet pulsed—soft, stubborn—like it didn't believe her.

And maybe, somewhere deep beneath the shadows— Neither did she.

***

The Beyond—a realm suspended between life and death, woven from threads of starlight and shadow. There is no ground beneath Rhylen's feet, no sky above, only an endless expanse of shimmering white and gold, like the fabric of existence itself stretched thin. The air hums with a quiet song, ancient and eternal, vibrating not through his ears but through his very soul.

Rhylen drifts in the nothingness, weightless.

There's no pain here. No grief. No shadow.

Just silence.

At first, he welcomes it. After everything—after *her*—the quiet feels like a mercy. But even here, beyond the reach of time, something stirs in the hollow places of his heart. A memory. A promise. A name.

Morganna.

Her face flickers behind his closed eyes—not the Queen of Shadows she became, but the girl with fierce determination and a stubborn tilt to her smile. The one who laughed like she wasn't afraid of breaking, even when she was.

The ache returns.

Rhylen opens his eyes.

In front of him stands a figure woven from pure light, impossible to define. Its shape shifts—sometimes tall, sometimes small, sometimes with wings, sometimes just a glow suspended in the vastness. There is no face, but he feels it watching him. Not with judgment. Not with pity.

With... something else.

Understanding.

The Light speaks—not with words, but with a voice that resonates through every fractured piece of him.

"You have done all you could."

Rhylen swallows hard, his throat dry despite the absence of breath. "It wasn't enough."

The Light doesn't argue. It doesn't need to. The truth is carved into Rhylen's bones, stitched into the spaces where guilt lives.

"Few are given the chance to return." The Light pulses softly, like a heartbeat. "But fate is not as rigid as Morgath believes. There is a thread, fragile and unfinished. It leads back to her. And to you."

Rhylen's chest tightens. Hope is more painful than grief.

"Back to Morganna?" His voice cracks on her name.

"Yes."

His heart—if he still has one here—stumbles over the weight of that word. But the Light isn't finished.

"You will not return as you were. To save her, you must be reborn."

Rhylen's brow furrows. "Reborn?"

"As one of the Fated Twelve." The Light's glow shifts, showing faint outlines of twelve intertwined threads stretching into the void, each pulsing with faint sparks—some bright, some flickering, some nearly extinguished. "Your path will not be easy. You will not remember everything—not until you meet the soul destined to awaken what was left behind."

His pulse roars in his ears—or maybe it's just the echo of what it used to be.

"You're saying I'll forget her?" His voice is sharp, bitter. The idea of not remembering *Morganna*, of letting her slip away even in his own mind, feels worse than death.

"Not forever. The heart remembers what the mind forgets. And when the time comes, you will know."

Rhylen closes his eyes. The emptiness feels heavier now, pressing against him from all sides.

He could stay. Let go. Rest.

But then he sees *her* again—not Morgath, not the shadow queen, but the girl who braided her hair with star charms, who believed in impossible things, who fought with everything she had even when it hurt.

I should've saved you.

His hands curl into fists, even though there's nothing to hold onto here.

"I'm not done," he whispers. Then louder, stronger—*himself*: "I'm not done."

The Light pulses again, brighter this time, as if smiling.

"Then choose."

Rhylen doesn't hesitate.

"I choose to go back."

The Light reaches toward him—or maybe *he* reaches toward *it*. Their connection blurs, golden threads wrapping around his form, pulling him into something vast and infinite.

"When you find your fated love, you will remember your purpose. Not just to save her... but to live. To love. For yourself."

The words ripple through him, soft and sharp all at once.

Rhylen feels himself unraveling—thread by thread, memory by memory—until all that's left is the *heartbeat*.

Then—

Darkness. A breath. A cry.

He is reborn.

Epilogue

"Fate does not forget, even when the world does. The past may shatter, but the echoes remain—waiting to be heard, waiting to return."
Centuries after the Heartstone shattered...

***

Far beyond the reach of Morgath's shadow, past the fractured lands and the broken echoes of the Weave, a single shard of light pulsed quietly in the darkness.

It had been hidden well—buried beneath the roots of the Eldergrove, where ancient trees whispered in languages older than time. The shard thrummed faintly, like a heartbeat beneath stone and soil, untouched by the corruption that seeped through the veins of Elysoria.

Until now.

The moment Morgath turned from the shattered mirror, her fury rippling through the fabric of the realms like a storm unleashed, the splinter awoke.

A flicker of golden light danced against the earth, fragile yet unyielding. The magic woven into it had been dormant for centuries, but prophecy was patient. The Heartstone had shattered, yes—but its pieces still remembered what it was.

And who it was meant to protect.

***

Somewhere in Elysoria, a baby takes his first breath under a sky streaked with faint threads of gold. A fragment of light flickers behind his newborn eyes—dormant, waiting.

Waiting for the girl who will remind him of who he is. Of who he *was*. And of the promise he made in the space between worlds.

I'm not done.

In a small village nestled on the border of the Duskwind Expanse, far from the echo of the Citadel's fallen glory, a child awoke from a dream.

Sweat clung to his brow, breath ragged, heart racing with fear and something else—something ancient.

The dream had been vivid: A sky ripped apart by shadow. A woman cloaked in darkness, her eyes burning like twin suns eclipsed. And a voice, soft but unyielding, speaking words the child had never heard before—

"Twelve hearts entwined the darkness break."

The words lingered in the air even after the dream had faded.

The child sat up, glancing out the window toward the distant mountains where the sky pulsed faintly with an unnatural light. The world was shifting, though they didn't yet understand why.

As dawn broke, they packed a small bag and slipped out of the village, drawn by an inner compass they couldn't explain.

The first of the prophesied Twelve had awakened, setting in motion events that would shape the fate of Elysoria.

***

Back in the Shadow Realm, Morgath stood at the precipice of her obsidian citadel, the void swirling around her like a living thing.

She felt it. The shift. The pulse of the splinter.

A disturbance in the shadows—a tiny spark of defiant light.

Her eyes narrowed, gaze sharp enough to cut stone. She thought back to the shards slipping through her fingers—pieces of power she thought she'd claimed, now scattered beyond her reach.

"So," she whispered to the darkness, *"the Heartstone still dares to defy me."*

Kaelith appeared beside her, his form more shadow than flesh, his grin sharp as broken glass. When he looked at her he saw the bracelet, and for a moment, that grin faltered.

"Balance always finds a way," he murmured, his voice like velvet and venom. *"It stirs. The first of the Twelve."*

Morgath knew of what he spoke, the prophecy she had glimpsed before -

"When shadows rise and the dragon wakes, Twelve hearts entwined the darkness break.

From flame and water, earth and air, From dreams and light, the bond they share.

Through love's pure spark, the soul shall mend, The shadow queen will meet her end.

Yet slivers of light within her dwell, For love transcends the darkest spell.

And twelve as one will seal the fate, To save the realms before too late."

Morgath's fingers twitched, her magic coiling around her wrists like serpents. The bracelet pulsed once—faint, stubborn.

She ignored it.

"Let them rise," she said softly, her smile brittle and cold. *"I will break them one by one."*

Her gaze drifted to the horizon, where the thin, fragile thread of light had dared to awaken.

"Hope," she whispered, tasting the word like poison on her tongue. *"Let's see how long it lasts."*

***

In the corners of the world, the remainder of the Fated Twelve stirred. Some as children born under strange stars. Some as warriors marked by scars that never healed. Some as outcasts, their destinies hidden beneath layers of doubt and fear.

But all of them were connected. Bound by threads Morgath had failed to sever. By love she had tried to destroy. By fate she had sworn to unravel.

And though she had shattered the Heartstone, fate had been waiting.

Somewhere deep inside the void, beneath all the rage and shadow and ruin— A sliver of her still remained. Bound to a bracelet she could not destroy. A bracelet woven with threads of light, darkness, and something in between.

Given to her with a star charm. A gift of friendship. A promise of love. Bound to her with hope.

***

"Let them come," she breathed into the void.

Her magic flared, summoning Umbraethyr from the depths of shadow, the great dragon's violet eyes gleaming with hunger.

Her lips curled into a smile—a cruel, beautiful thing.

"And I will show them what happens when love tries to fight the dark."

The shadows rose. The prophecy awakened. And the war for fate had only just begun.

Dear Reader,

From the depths of my heart—thank you.

Thank you for stepping into the world of *Whispers in the Weave*, for following Morganna's journey, for embracing the magic, the heartbreak, and the whispers of fate.

This story is more than just words on a page. It's for those who have ever felt torn between light and shadow, between who they are and who they're meant to be. It's for the ones who have loved, lost, and still found the courage to rise again.

Your time, your imagination, and your belief in this story mean everything. Whether this book made you feel something, made you dream, or simply gave you a place to escape for a while—I am grateful.

If you enjoyed *Whispers in the Weave*, I would love to hear your thoughts! Reviews help stories like this find their way to more readers, and your words mean more than you know.

You are part of this journey now. And the Weave always remembers.

With love and endless gratitude, Joceline Sparx

***

"The greatest villains were once the greatest dreamers—until the world gave them a reason to break."

***

Want to stay connected? Join me for exclusive updates, behind-the-scenes looks, and more magical adventures: www.jocelinesparx.com

About the Author: Joceline Sparx

Joceline Sparx is a writer of dark fantasy, swoon-worthy romance, and morally gray characters who refuse to stay in their lanes. When she's not weaving tales of epic love, shadowed destinies, and magic gone terribly wrong, she can be found tucked away in a cozy cabin deep in the woods, where the whisper of the trees sounds suspiciously like story ideas. Her loyal (and enormous) writing companion, Koda, an Anatolian Pyrenees with the heart of a guardian and the fluff of an overgrown cloud, keeps her company during late-night writing sessions and long walks beneath the towering pines. Joceline's obsessions include: Wandering the woods like she's on a quest. Binge-reading paranormal romance and urban fantasy until reality fades. Chai tea in dangerous quantities, because caffeine is basically a magical potion. Sketching characters when words aren't enough to capture them. Binge-watching shows like *Teen Wolf*, *Haven*, *Lost Girl*, and *Grimm*—because nothing beats supernatural drama with just the right amount of angst. She believes every story should have a touch of magic, a dash of heartbreak, and characters who feel like they could step right off the page (or punch you in the face, depending on their mood).

Follow Joceline Sparx for more dark, enchanting tales filled with fierce heroines, brooding anti-heroes, and the kind of romances that linger long after the last page. www.jocelinesparx.com

***

"Stories are where we become immortal—where love, loss, and destiny are rewritten with every turn of the page."

Acknowledgments

No story is ever woven alone, and *Whispers in the Weave* would not exist without the love, support, and encouragement of some truly incredible people. To my husband, for always believing in me, even when I doubted myself. For the patience, the late-night brainstorming sessions, and for reminding me to take breaks when I get lost in my worlds. I love you endlessly. To Heather, Katrina, Alanna, Emmalei, Tna, and Merri—your support, inspiration, and friendship mean more than I can ever put into words. Thank you for listening to my wild ideas, for cheering me on when the doubts crept in, and for always being a part of my journey. To every reader, dreamer, and believer in fate and love—thank you for stepping into this world with me. Your time, your imagination, and your heart are what truly bring this story to life. May the Weave always whisper to you.

With gratitude,

Joceline Sparx

***

"No story is woven alone. Every thread, every voice, every heartbeat adds to the tapestry. Thank you for being part of mine."

Introduction to the Shadowed Enchantment Series
By Joceline Sparx

"When shadows rise and the dragon wakes, Twelve hearts entwined the darkness break."

Every story begins with a spark. Sometimes it's hope. Sometimes it's vengeance. And sometimes—it's a love so fierce it refuses to be forgotten, even by the gods themselves.

Welcome to the world of *Shadowed Enchantment*, where love isn't just a feeling—it's magic, stitched into the very fabric of fate. Long ago, Morganna the Luminous—the brightest of the Guardians—fell. She shattered the Heartstone, the source of all balance, and became Morgath, the Queen of Shadows.

Her grief twisted into rage. Her love into obsession. Her power into a curse that spread like a shadow across the realms. But fate is never truly broken. When the Heartstone shattered, it splintered into twelve fragments, hidden across Elysoria. Each shard carries a whisper of what was lost—and a promise of what could be restored.

The prophecy speaks of the *Fated Twelve*—pairs of souls bound not just by destiny, but by love strong enough to challenge the darkness itself. Their stories are not the same. Some will fight for kingdoms. Some will fight for freedom. Some will fight simply to survive. But in the end, they are all connected. Twelve shards. Twelve souls. Twelve chances to rewrite the ending Morgath thought she had sealed. This isn't a love story. It's twelve.

Each book in the *Shadowed Enchantment* series is a standalone tale—fierce, magical, and wildly romantic—but together, they weave the tapestry of an epic battle between light and shadow. Between fate and choice. Between the love that was lost... and the love that might just save the world. The prophecy has already begun. The shadows are rising. And somewhere out there, a piece of the story belongs to you. Are you ready to find it?

***

"The Weave remembers. The echoes remain. And the next thread has already begun to unravel..."

Shadowed Enchantments Series Sneak Peak

The journey is only beginning...You've walked the path of fate with *Whispers in the Weave*, witnessing the fall of a legend and the birth of a shadow. But the echoes of destiny are far from over. The world of Elysoria still trembles under Morgath's curse, and across its enchanted lands, twelve fated love stories are waiting to unfold. Each tale weaves together dark magic, forbidden romance, and the power of love against impossible odds. Welcome to the *Shadowed Enchantments* series—where fairy tales are reborn in darkness, desire, and destiny.

***

The Fated Twelve

Book 1: The Curse of Crowns (Beauty and the Beast reimagined) A prince bound to a cursed crown that drains his very life. A forbidden sorceress seeking the truth behind the Eclipse Prophecy. When fate brings them together, they uncover the echoes of a forgotten past, a prophecy that could restore what was lost, and a love that defies the boundaries of time itself. But with darkness closing in and the weight of destiny upon them, will they break the curse—or be consumed by it?

Book 2: Enchanted Shadows (*Cinderella Reimagined*) A seamstress who weaves magic into her creations. A lord cursed to walk as a shadow by night. A forbidden love bound by secrets and spells.

Book 3: Whispering Woods (*Little Red Riding Hood Reimagined*) A huntress seeking vengeance. A brooding werewolf with a past soaked in blood. A forest where spirits whisper warnings and a Wolf King waits in the dark.

Book 4: Twisted Beauty (*Snow White Reimagined*) A sorceress exiled. A cursed prince bound in servitude. A stolen throne steeped in dark magic. Together, Isabella and Adrian must shatter an evil queen's hold on their fate—or be consumed by it.

Book 5: Veiled Midnight (*Sleeping Beauty Reimagined*) A dreamweaver trapped in a slumbering curse. A prince lost in the realm of nightmares. To awaken, they must navigate a world where fear is alive and shadows devour souls.

Book 6: Abyssal Tides (*The Little Mermaid Reimagined*) A siren princess exiled to the abyss. A cursed sea captain doomed to transform beneath the waves. The ocean hides ancient gods, forbidden magic, and a love that defies the tides.

Book 7: Swan's Veil (*The Swan Princess Reimagined*) A noblewoman cursed to become a swan by moonlight. A prince trapped in his own enchanted fate. Their love must break the spell—or be lost to the lake's depths forever.

Book 8: Tangled Whispers (*Rapunzel Reimagined*) A sorceress imprisoned in a tower of illusions. A rogue with a vendetta against the witch who holds her captive. Her hair binds her to fate, but his love may be the key to setting her free.

Book 9: Crimson Woods (*Goldilocks and the Three Bears Reimagined*) A witch who walks between dreams. Three bear brothers with elemental magic. A forbidden forest where love and danger intertwine.

Book 10: Maze of Moonlight (*Labyrinth Reimagined*) A sorceress forced to enter a living maze. A brooding guardian bound to its secrets. As illusions twist reality, their hearts become the only truth.

Book 11: Blade of Destiny (*The Princess Bride Reimagined*) A warrior seeking her lost love. A rogue with secrets written in blood. Their journey across enchanted lands will test their blades—and their hearts.

Book 12: Unicorn's Shadow (*Legend Reimagined*) A guardian of the last unicorn. A fallen knight consumed by shadows. Their bond could restore the balance between light and darkness—or doom the world to eternal night.

Finale: Eternal Ever After - Twelve couples. Twelve battles fought. And one final war to determine the fate of Elysoria. The Heartstone has shattered, but love may still have the power to rewrite fate.

Twelve fated pairs. Twelve epic journeys. One final reckoning. Fate demands obedience—will you dare to defy it?

The *Shadowed Enchantments* series is waiting.

Follow Joceline Sparx for updates, exclusive content, and release dates! www.jocelinesparx.com

The Hollow Crown
Sneak Peek

"You don't remember me, do you?"

Elara's voice was barely a whisper, but it cut through the heavy silence like a blade. She stood at the edge of the stone dais, the flickering torchlight painting golden shadows across her face—across the soft curve of her jaw, the determined set of her mouth, the wild defiance in her golden eyes.

Dorian's grip tightened on the hilt of his sword, the Hollow Crown burning against his temples.

The curse pulsed, as if it recognized her—even if he didn't.

"I don't know you," he ground out, though something inside him twisted at the lie.

Elara took a slow step forward, the chains at her wrists clinking softly.

"You do. Somewhere deep inside, beneath all of this."

She gestured toward the dark thorns wrapped around his head.

"You've just forgotten." The air thickened with tension—magic hummed between them, raw and crackling.

"You have three days, sorceress," Dorian growled.

"Break my curse or hang from the pyre."

But Elara didn't flinch. She smiled—small, sad, knowing—and in that moment, something ancient stirred inside him.

"I'm not here to break your curse, Dorian," she whispered.

"I'm here to remind you who you really are."

And then, as the torches guttered low, he heard it—a voice from a life he couldn't quite remember."

Rhylen... you promised me forever."

The Hollow Crown cracked—just a hairline fracture—but enough for the darkness to notice. And enough for fate to finally begin unraveling.

The past isn't dead. It's just waiting to be remembered.

Coming soon: ***The Hollow Crown***

Where fate is fractured, magic is forbidden, and not all monsters can be slain.

www.ingramcontent.com/pod-product-compliance
Lightning Source LLC
LaVergne TN
LVHW041702060526
838201LV00043B/539